LIANG WERN FOOK is a writer, musician, singer, and professor of Chinese literature. During the 1980s, he played a pivotal role as one of the pioneering figures in the xinyao movement, which celebrated Singaporean Chinese folk songs. He has received numerous awards across diverse artistic genres, including the prestigious Singapore Cultural Medallion. With a prolific body of work, he boasts over twenty publications spanning various creative genres and an impressive repertoire of more than three hundred songs. Widely recognised for his ability to blend literature and music, his works have left an indelible mark on Singapore's vibrant art scene.

CHRISTINA NG is a Singaporean writer, journalist and translator based in Berlin. Her Chinese to English translations include poetry by Singaporean poets Liang Wern Fook, Ting Kheng Siong, Dan Ying and Chinese poet Hua Qing.

Balestier Press
Centurion House, London TW18 4AX
1010 Dover Road #01-800, Singapore 139658
www.balestier.com

The Joy of a Left Hand
Original title: 左手的快乐
Original text © Liang Wern Fook
English translation © Christina Ng, 2023

English translation arranged with Global Publishing, an imprint of
World Scientific Publishing Co. Pte Ltd., Singapore.

English edition first published by Balestier Press in 2023

Published with the support of

NATIONAL ARTS COUNCIL
SINGAPORE

A CIP catalogue record for this book is available from the British Library.

ISBN 978 1 913891 55 8

Edited by Tiffany Tsao
Cover design by Sarah and Schooling

This book is a work of fiction. The literary perceptions and insights are based
on experience, all names, characters, places, and incidents either are products
of the author's imagination or are used fictitiously.

LIANG WERN FOOK

THE JOY OF A LEFT HAND

Translated from the Chinese by
Christina Ng

BALESTIER PRESS
LONDON · SINGAPORE

Contents

A DAY IN HISTORY

Confucius sits in his chair with his back straight as a ramrod, a copy of *The Chunqiu Annals* lying on the table before him. He rivets his attention on the book as a familiar voice behind him whispers, 'Go on. Edit it.'

He sighs, takes an ink brush and crosses out a whole paragraph.

After a while, he hears the same voice softly urging him again: 'Keep editing!'

The expression on Confucius's face is one of pain and helplessness as he crosses out another paragraph, puts down his brush, and sighs again.

The whisper behind him turns up its volume: 'Okay, let's call it a day. It's a wrap!'

After issuing the order, the director walks up to the actor who has been playing the role of Confucius in the show. 'I'm just in love with that expression of yours; it's so unique! That depth, that profundity—it says it all about history!'

Their collaboration dynamic has been seamless since they've started working together on this TV series, *A Day in History*. In fact, everyone has even fallen into calling the actor by his character's name.

The director puts his hand on Confucius's shoulder and asks if he'd like to grab a drink. Just then, another director walks up to them and asks: 'Could you help me out? Can you direct Confucius here to edit *Chunqiu* again? I need to do a pickup shot.'

This next director has been shooting *A Day in History: Behind the Scenes* with his crew on the side. He starts to instruct the first director, telling him how he should be directing Confucius in his editing of *Chunqiu*.

The first director smiles wryly. 'This isn't the way I direct a show. I'd never do this! Where are all the shots you got just now? Haven't you filmed, like, a lot?'

The next director continues filming his pickup shots. 'Well, this shot is exactly how I want to present *Behind the Scenes*. I've edited out those other shots I filmed. Anyway, you've also edited out a lot of shots with Confucius in them. And don't get me started on how even Confucius has been editing a lot of his own expressions.'

During the back and forth between the two directors, all the needed pickup shots are finally completed. Confucius, the director of *A Day in History*, as well as the director of *A Day in History: Behind the Scenes* head off for drinks together.

The people who arrive next pay the bill.

HOLD IT IN

He walks into the gents and finds it filled with men, peeing. He unzips his trousers and is about to pee when all the men in the bathroom start to sing. Overcome with shock, he holds it in.

His wife is sound asleep beside him when he opens his eyes. He sits up, cutting a solitary figure in the middle of the night. His thoughts wander to the excursion he and his wife, together with his son's family, made to Clarke Quay the night before.

Clarke Quay had changed so much that he felt that he was in another country—not that he's ever left Singapore's shores. They walked to the small circular plaza in the centre of Clarke Quay where several people were onstage singing English songs.

'This place is a toilet, you know!' he insisted to his son. 'Back in the day, every time I cycle past here, I always stop and go in to pee.'

'Grandpa,' his young grandson chimed in. 'Cannot say "pee"! It's rude! When Daddy and Mummy take me to other countries, the tour guide always say, "Let's go sing song!" when it's time to go toilet.'

His daughter-in-law shushed the little boy, telling him to stop blabbering and concentrate on the songs the people were singing. He, on the other hand, was confused, unsure if his daughter-in-law was talking to him or his grandson. The crowd was deeply enthralled by the singing. But all he wanted to do was scream, 'THIS PLACE IS A TOILET!'

He gets out of bed. Roused from her sleep, his wife asks drowsily, 'What's wrong?'

He exclaims in no uncertain tone, 'I've held it in the whole night. Now I must go sing song!'

DRIP

The spouse is on top of her.

It's been a while since he's lasted this long. Tonight, he is like a man charged with cautious excitement, labouring away to make the act last as long as he can, his moves slow and deliberate from the start.

Ever since they got married, the spouse has always taken the top position. This has been the status quo for as long as she can remember, and she's always gone along with it without so much as a squeak. At first, she was merely bashful. But, as time went by, the meekness became indifference. She often feels limp, like a deflated balloon, so taking the bottom position means that not much effort is needed on her part.

She's been tired for as long as she can remember. Every single day, there are household chores to do. She doesn't understand why the more chores she does, the more they multiply, with no end in sight! The spouse's waistline, likewise, has continued to expand. Every time he's on top, her mind wanders to the housework stacked up, like a towering block, pressing her down and leaving her sapped of energy.

The spouse now closes his eyes and pants softly. This reminds her of every single time he's been unwilling to lift a finger when she asks if he can share the heavy load of household chores. She has never seen him exert an ounce of effort, not even when he had to train for the physical fitness test at his annual reservist call-up.

Now she can see it—a drop of sweat—an extremely slow accumulation of tiny droplets on the spouse's nose.

One. Big. Drop.

A drop so crystal clear because he's so near.

She begins to worry about the bead of sweat sliding down the length of his nose and falling onto her face. It wasn't easy for her to finally finish washing her face and slather on moisturiser, just as, earlier in the day, it hadn't been easy to finally finish handwashing some clothes. With tremendous effort, she'd wrung them dry, hung them on the heavy bamboo pole, heaved the pole to the kitchen, and then slotted the flagpole-like, horizontal row of clothes into a pipe socket outside the kitchen window to bake them in the sun. They'd been drying beautifully until a steady trickle of water from the flat upstairs started to fall, wetting her beloved clothes.

It happened every single time. Whenever the clothes had almost soaked up all the sunshine, drops of water from the flat above would threaten to undo the sun's work.

Now the spouse, on top of her, starts to moan softly. She can't stand it any longer. This morning, she finally plucked up enough courage to walk upstairs and knock on the door. No one answered, so she tried the doorbell, pressing it again and again. Someone shouted from inside, 'Coming!' The window slid open. A man popped his head out. She suddenly recalled seeing him before in the lift, always immaculately dressed in a suit and tie for work. She beheld his bare upper body, damp with sweat as he huffed and puffed upon reaching the window, where he leaned his mop against the frame.

'What's the matter?' asked the man.

Ah, so this was her upstairs neighbour!

'Where's your wife?' she asked.

'Not home. What's up?'

'Your clothes aren't dry. The water always drips onto my clothes.'

'Auntie, it's like this when you live in an HDB flat.'

'But, we're neighbours!'

'Auntie, since I'm living on top and you below, just smile and take it easy lah.'

'I don't know what you mean by who's on top and who's below.'

'I mean, if you don't like it, get yourself an upgrade,' he retorted. 'Go live in an executive condominium. Get yourself a loft garden while you're at it.'

From where he stood at the window, the man looked like he was leisurely scratching something below his waist. She couldn't make out what he was doing, but she couldn't pretend not to see it either. Meanwhile, the bead of sweat balancing precariously on the spouse's nose looks like it's going to fall on her any minute now. The spouse is on top of her, his body glistening with sweat.

Her upstairs neighbour continued: 'You should go live in a bungalow. Then nobody will be living above you, so you won't feel hot and bothered.'

The spouse now seems to be hot and invigorated, his moves quickening. She's noticed the spouse has become more and more engaged in sporting activities as such. Once, she had brought up the constant problem of the dripping clothes with her close friends and one of them advised her to file a complaint. 'You should consider it. Singapore is all about law and order!' the friend had said.

Now, the bead of sweat is making more progress down the spouse's nose, threatening to splatter her any time. Her thoughts start to wander to the possibility of filing a complaint in court.

'You want to complain, is it?' her upstairs neighbour said when she'd confronted him. 'Go ahead and complain. At most, people will come over to my place to check. I bet they won't be dropping by your place every day waiting for the water from my clothes to drip on yours, though. Then again, if you want to complain, go ahead. Complain your head off. Just don't waste my time.' He slid his window shut.

She was overcome with weariness—a weariness that had been dragging her down for some time. Where would she go to make a complaint? Was it worthwhile? The thought of complaining and having people over to check made her even more tired. It brought to mind what another close friend once said about something else—that there were people who didn't even get a chance to engage in 'sporting activities.' 'You should be grateful,' said the friend. 'When a man initiates, it's because he wants to give his woman a good time.'

At the time, those words had only reminded her of her spouse's unending complaints about having to go back to camp for reservist military drills. 'I can't wait for time to pass faster!' he would groan. Why did she share the same feeling about housework? Each and every time, she couldn't wait for the task to be over once she'd started. She always tried her best to be quick about it. Anyhow, she should try to make love happen during the bedroom chore.

Chop-chop, go back downstairs and bring the clothes back into the flat, she told herself. Before she went upstairs this morning, she'd left the clothes on the bamboo pole to prove they were bespattered with water. She would probably have to wash them all over again.

Quick. Get it over and done with.

At that moment, the spouse moans, 'Coming...' Her upstairs neighbour had muttered 'coming' when he slid his window open, annoyance oozing out of every pore. Afterwards, upon reaching her door and hearing the phone in her flat ringing ceaselessly, she had wanted to yell, 'Coming!' as well. But the ringing stopped as soon as she'd let herself in. Her thoughts had been fully occupied by the clothes then. Chop-chop, bring them in. Good grief, the water was still dripping from upstairs, and the red shirt's colour seemed to be running this time. Drop by drop it dripped.

Coming.

Now, the bead of sweat travels its final length towards her. She can see it large and clear. From the tip of the spouse's nose, inching towards her face below him—the bloated blob of sweat looms so, so close.

'Coming!' she screams, in tandem with the person on top.

CHASTITY

'…' she mumbled, her head down. She had no inkling what she was trying to say. Her boyfriend continued to fumble with the first button of her blouse as he whispered her name.

'…' she murmured, feeling ill at ease, her head still down. Her boyfriend moved his fingers to the second button. Suddenly, she looked up and pushed his hand away. She buttoned up her blouse and said in a clearer, albeit tremulous, voice, 'No.'

*

While her students were working on their compositions, the single, bespectacled teacher in her thirties let her mind drift back to the previous night. Her thoughts were interrupted when a young girl in the front row asked a question.

'Miss, how do I write the Chinese characters for zhēncāo?'

Her heart pounded on hearing that word, as if a raw nerve had been touched. She replied in a low voice, 'What did you say?'

The girl had always been shy, and had never dared to ask a question in front of the whole class. She'd kept her head down as usual when she'd asked the question. Her voice was a murmur, tremulous. 'How do I write the Chinese characters for zhēncāo?' she asked again.

The female teacher couldn't believe her ears. She looked around the class and saw everyone else, heads lowered in concentration, working hard on their compositions. She lowered her voice further, enunciating each word: 'Say. That. Again. Be clearer, please.'

The female student looked up, and asked in a voice as clear as a bell, 'How do I write the Chinese characters for zhēngchāo?'

The female teacher felt her heart heave a sigh of relief. Her ears had indeed played a trick on her. She wrote the two Chinese characters for the word 'quarrel' (zhēngchāo) on a small piece of paper and handed it to the girl. She returned to grading her pile of homework assignments.

The young girl copied the two characters into her exercise book and continued her composition.

The small piece of paper lying on the young girl's desk still bore traces of the female teacher's erased scrawl: 'chastity' – 贞操 (zhēncāo).

THE DAY UNCLE SPOKE

It had to have been the silliest thing I'd done in my whole life. I realised it when I flipped through the papers the next day, and it dawned on me that I'd actually jostled my way into a crowd of at least twenty thousand people to watch the firecrackers going off.

Though 'watch' wasn't quite the right word. I didn't even catch a glimpse of a firecracker—only heard a faint series of pops and crackles from afar.

Anyway, I didn't really care. As a kid, I'd never once heard of such a thing as a firecracker, which explains my nonchalance. As a matter of fact, for the past thirty-four years, no one in this country has ever heard these bangers with their own ears. But now I've heard them all right.

Perhaps that's why my Chinese teacher capitalised on our brand-new discovery and gave us a special writing assignment: How does the younger generation feel about setting off, um, no, *watching* firecrackers being set off?

However, to a firecracker newbie like me, the most exciting part of that day wasn't the firecrackers but taking my uncle out on my own for the very first time.

Mum said, 'You want to go, don't you? Grandma can't walk very well, and I've got to work overtime. So why don't you take your uncle to watch the firecrackers instead?'

Uncle (that's Mum's brother by the way) was almost forty. When I grew old enough to make sense of the world, I realised that I'd never seen him step out of the house. He doesn't speak, so the family feels uneasy about letting him head out alone. As Grandma got on in years, his chances of getting out of the house grew even slimmer. He became resigned to staying at home with Grandma, sitting by her side and watching television with her for days on end.

To this day, I still don't know why Uncle doesn't speak. I'm not sure if he can't talk, doesn't want to talk, or is unable to talk. Despite all my speculations, I do know that he wasn't born mute;

he could speak when he was a child.

Grandma had told me the story umpteen times before, although I'd never understood a word of what she would say. She used some language that Mum and her spoke. In contrast, Mum only had to tell me the story in English once and I understood everything immediately.

'One Chinese New Year, when Uncle was small, a neighbour's child chucked a banger at him. Your Uncle screamed and got badly burnt. After that, we've never heard him utter so much as a squeak.'

Every Chinese New Year, Grandma would tell this story all over again in that language I didn't understand. Nodding my head, I would pretend to comprehend everything she was saying. She must have seen right through me, but she never exposed me. I didn't expose her either, even though she would sit in front of the TV watching the news and soap operas in Mandarin without understanding a single word.

Uncle would always sit next to Grandma, watching television with her. I wasn't sure if he understood anything of what he watched either. After all, I'd never heard him utter a single word. It didn't really matter, since I couldn't understand anything that my Grandma's side of the family said. Uncle usually spoke to me through gestures, which turned out to be a better way for us to communicate.

In truth, if it wasn't for Uncle using hand gestures to tell me how much he wanted me to take him to Tang Ren Jie—oops, I mean Niu Che Shui (Bullock Cart Water)—I wouldn't have cared to go. (My Chinese teacher said that we shouldn't use the word Tang Ren Jie in Chinese to refer to Chinatown, since it's the verbatim word-for-word translation of 'Chinatown' that the English papers like to use.)

In any case, it was my first time there, and would probably be my last. The place was jam-packed. Thanks to the crowds, I couldn't see any of the firecracker action, except for hordes of police officers keeping order.

I did, however, see something truly special—saw and heard, in fact. When the firecrackers were busy crackling in the distance and the twenty thousand people hushed up, their mouths agape, I saw Uncle, who was next to me, suddenly open his mouth and exclaim, 'AH!'

I was surrounded by swarms and swarms of people. But not one of them heard my uncle. Not even the police officers who were there maintaining order.

I wonder if anyone there that day felt a tug on their heartstrings like I did. Was there a tiny yank in their chests? A wee pull that caused little wells of tears to spring up in their eyes? Tears that trickled down their faces as they watched the firecrackers go ping, bang, bang?

I didn't get all soppy, of course. I tried my best to keep my cool since the place was already filled with wild excitement. So I didn't react to my uncle's first word in a long time. Apparently, there's a Chinese idiom for this kind of situation: ting er bu wen, which means 'to turn a deaf ear'. I remember it because I got an A on my Chinese exam.

To me, Uncle had spoken that day. I came to that conclusion, for that gasp of 'AH' was speech to me. If he had babbled on in that language that Grandma speaks, I wouldn't have understood a single word.

When we got home, I didn't mention a word of it to my Mum and Grandma. Mum asked if the firecrackers display was good, and I said it would've been better if we'd watched it on TV.

Uncle never spoke again after that day. And I've never been back to Chinatown. Um, sorry—I mean Niu Che Shui. You know. Bullock Cart Water.

FINANCIAL SUPPORT

I have a friend who works at a national cultural history museum. One of his job responsibilities is to collect exhibits. He amasses items from the previous century, that is, 'cultural artifacts' from before the year 2000. Every time I visit him at his office for a lunch date, I'm able to find something interesting in his basket of 'disqualified' items.

Today, I managed to find two interesting items in that basket again.

The first was an invitation, which went like this:

Presentation of monthly cheque to my mother, on (date) of (month), 19xx, same procedure as every year
You are cordially invited to a presentation ceremony of this month's cheque to my mother.
Light refreshments will be served.
We look forward to your attendance.
Banquet Venue: xx Restaurant
With best wishes,
Mr. xx and Wife

The second item I found was a 'Letter of Advice' sent by a lawyer's office.

Dear Mr. xx:
We are writing in regard to the monthly acknowledgement slips that you have been sending us. They confirm your receipt of the monthly cheques that have been kindly provided by your son to assist you in your old age. We hereby implore you to take note of two things:
1. Please keep to a standardised way of signing your name, so as not to bring any undue inconvenience to the officer in charge of your case.
2. Please refrain from writing things like 'I miss you so much' on the

acknowledgement slip.
Thank you.
Yours sincerely,
XXX
DD.MM. YYYY

I asked my friend what these documents were. He shrugged and replied, 'Useless items.' He then proceeded to throw the card and letter back into the basket and, putting his hand on my shoulder, led me out of the office for lunch.

AMBER

Amber walked into the study room, leaned over my shoulder and read aloud the words in the magazine that I was reading.

'The rich and abundant amber found on Hispaniola Island in the Caribbean was originally resin from a Hymenaea Tree…'

I caught a whiff of fragrance in Amber's hair, a scent that reminded me of a certain flower. Momentarily distracted, my attention strayed from the magazine that I was poring over, and I looked up to plant a kiss on her perfumed neck.

'Ah! Now I know why this place is called Hymanaea Park!' Amber exclaimed. 'Then again, don't you think it's strange to name a residence after a tree that doesn't exist anymore?' She wondered this aloud in a girly voice as I put my arm around her waist.

I didn't say a word. My lips sought out her lips, responding to her tongue with the answer lying thick and indolent on mine. As she moaned beneath me, my mind, to my astonishment, went over the sentences I'd just read in the magazine.

'Insects, crawling bugs, bird feathers as well as flower petals etc. (I caught a whiff of floral fragrance again) *are often caught in the resin of the Hymenaea Tree. As the resin acts as a sort of sticky trap, whatever is caught within will be perfectly preserved.*

'I'm so tired,' whispered Amber, chest heaving softly, back against the floor, eyes on the ceiling.

'Mm.' My eyes were half-closed. The fragrance of flower petals drifted into my nose.

'I don't know why, but I've been losing a lot of hair recently. My skin seems to be losing its colour too,' she said before falling into a deep sleep.

I sat up and looked at her, sound asleep beside me. As I sat there listening to the rhythmic rise and fall of her breath, it was as if the colour was trickling out of her as her breath ebbed away. At the same time, her floral fragrance was fading like a receding tide.

I stood up and went to my desk to look up the article in the magazine. Even though the article was on biology, I found it to be as stimulating as poetry.

'*Amber is an everlasting time capsule. It is a world that has vanished.*'

I picked up my pen and started to write Amber a letter.

Dear Amber,

I've never told you this. You must know that it's not just you, but also me who has been losing hair in this house. In fact, I'm losing colour too. Sometimes, I notice hair belonging to you and me entangled on the floor, and I get this feeling that those strands of hair are parts of us, intertwined.

I've always believed that if I kept you carefully wrapped up in the golden light of the setting sun of that year, you'd be encased in my memory. It would be just like sparkling golden amber, clear in its shimmer, wrapping itself around a flower petal like it was its eternal finery.

That's why I decided not to read the news, about how you died in a car accident the day after we said goodbye to each other. I refused to attend your funeral. They said I was heartless, but little did they know how deep my love for you was. From that day on, they thought of me as a person unscarred, moving on with life and growing old with scarcely a dent in his heart. They didn't see the other me, the one who would often escape into this other world that no longer exists. In this world, you stopped growing old that day, that year. As for me, I've clung on to you—this eternal you. I was determined to stop the story of my life from casting out my youth.

I created Hymenaea Park and the eternal Amber within. But I neglected one of Nature's laws: anything built with human hands will vanish one day. Unlike natural amber, which preserves the original form of a living thing for millions of years, the amber of my creation isn't able to withstand the test of time. External forces didn't destroy this version of you. But I have. I've slowly let you fade away. I've even let myself fade away, the me you knew from that year.

Amber, I don't have many more years left in me. The few years I've been left with have become a house to shelter my memory. It's filled with the woe of waiting—waiting for the youthful you and me to fade, and vanish.

Now, I'm going to leave Hymenaea Park for the last time. I'm never going to come back. I don't know if you'll be upset when you wake up. But I know I can no longer endure the hopelessness of both of us entwined together, losing our shape and colour—both of us, coming to a brutal end, disappearing without a trace.

Farewell, Amber. I love you.

WHAT SHOULD I DO?

'Mum? Am I really a human being? Or am I actually a robot?'

This is what I overheard my grandson ask my daughter in the courtyard ablaze in the light of the penetrating morning sun. Children of this age love asking adults all kinds of strange questions.

'Of course you're human. I gave birth to you, so how can you be a robot?' my daughter explained patiently to my grandson. I walked away after that, not wanting to intrude on their private moment. It's important for a mother and son to trust each other; outsiders shouldn't meddle in their affairs.

'Dad. My kid asked if he was a robot this morning,' my daughter said.

We were back in the house, its four corners ablaze in the penetrating light of the evening sun.

'How did you answer him?'

'I told him he's a real person made of flesh and blood, of course.'

The sun ran its bright fingers over my daughter's face, as if pointing out to me how haggard she was. The day had probably exhausted her—she looked frazzled and distressed.

'But what if, one day, he realises that he really is a robot? What should I do?'

I didn't answer her. I was, instead, envious of her comparatively blissful state. She only had to worry about how to hide the truth from my grandson. But me? I'd never stopped worrying about the tower of consequences that would tumble down on me if my daughter ever realized that she, too, was a robot.

'Don't you have any advice for me? If he discovers the truth one day, what should I do?'

'I wouldn't know what to do either.'

'You must know. You know everything.'

'I really don't. I'm not even…'

I couldn't complete my sentence. A sudden wave of fear washed over me. What if, I mean, what if the author who created me thought that he was God, but turned out to be just a 'human being' that 'God' created? What should I do?

A TASTE OF NIANGAO

Uncle opened the door for me when I visited that day. As soon as he saw me, he blurted, 'And the niangao. Do you have the niangao?'

'Yes, I've got them here.'

This sort of back and forth had become a norm, practically a ritual that we had to perform before kicking off the Chinese New Year celebrations.

Ma and Pa couldn't come, so I was standing in for them to celebrate with Uncle the long tradition of sending away the old and ushering in the new. This time every year, I fly back from Guangzhou to Singapore. After being posted to China for work a few years ago, there haven't been many opportunities for me to visit family in Singapore. I often have to wait till the New Year—Spring Festival as they call it in China—where I get a much longer holiday than back home. Some people remark that spending Spring Festival in China—arguably a country with stronger Chinese New Year traditions and festive spirit than Singapore—might be more enjoyable. However, to me, Chinese New Year is a time when everyone goes home. Home, for me, is Singapore.

My uncle is getting on in years. He lives with my single cousin who works during the day, leaving him alone in the flat to while away the hours. I could tell he was thrilled to see me, as if he'd been fervently counting down to that one day when I, the most junior member of the family, would finally arrive at his door.

But of course, I knew what delighted him most was the niangao I would bring home from Guangzhou.

At the door, Uncle looked like age hadn't just caught up with him but hastened forward, cruelly pulling him along. He'd aged a lot since I'd seen him the year before. I'd heard from Ma and Pa that the two surgeries he'd undergone earlier this year had debilitated him, enfeebling him even more than before.

I hadn't even warmed my seat when Uncle gave voice to what was on the tip of his tongue—something he tended to repeat, over and over: 'Uncle's getting old. I'll have to go meet my maker very soon.'

'Uncle, stop saying that.'

'This whole year, I've told myself that I can only go after eating the niangao you bring me. I have to celebrate Chinese New Year with you. Then I can go in peace.'

'Uncle, I'm sure you'll always get to eat the niangao that I bring home every year.'

'Mm. So how's your Aunt doing?'

That was really the heart of my visit. The concern that dominated Uncle's mind every time I came was Aunt's wellbeing in Guangzhou.

'Aunt's doing very well. She wants me to tell you to take good care of yourself. And next year, you'll still be able to eat the niangao she asks me to bring.'

'Yes, the niangao. Ah, there's nothing like the niangao your Aunt makes! I've eaten so many kinds of niangao all these years, but none as good as hers.'

I listened patiently to Uncle, even though it wasn't the first time I'd heard him say these things. Old people love sifting through the memories lovingly stored at the back of their minds. It doesn't matter if it's a memory of Aunt's niangao, or him leaving my then young Aunt behind in their hometown for a new life in Singapore, or how Aunt got into a fluster trying to bake him niangao so he could eat them during his first Spring Festival in Nanyang, without her. Now he continued to unearth these precious mementos hoarded in the far reaches of his mind, showing them to me yet again: the war that broke out, the peace that ensued; the chaos that tore him and Aunt apart, resulting in them living in two different lands, cut off from each other.

'I did your Aunt wrong. I married a second woman here. May Heaven bless your Aunt with good health and happiness in old age.'

'Aunt doesn't blame you,' I said. And it wasn't a white lie.

A few years ago, I got in contact with some distant relatives in Guangzhou after a lot of asking around, and I finally found the Aunt that Uncle had been talking about day and night. When I met her, nothing suggested that she harboured a hint of resentment against Uncle. In truth, she was living reasonably well in her old age. To prove that she didn't blame Uncle, she even made me some niangao to bring back to him. I shouldn't tell Uncle that she'd made them, she instructed, for she wanted to know if he still remembered the taste of her niangao.

I'd brought them to him. And upon first bite, his eyes began to water, rivulets of tears streaming down to his chin.

'Your Aunt made this niangao with her own hands,' he had told me.

This time, Uncle was as hungry for the niangao as always. While we chatted, he stretched out his hand for one of the niangao in the gift basket. His fingers, trembling with excitement, started to cut a small slice. I tried to stop him.

'Uncle, you should stay away from sweet food.'

Uncle paid no attention to me and popped the niangao into his mouth. I sighed. He would still attempt to eat it when I left, even if I managed to stop him now.

He smacked his lips in satisfaction. 'Your Aunt's niangao is so special.'

Before I left, I said to Uncle, 'Take very good care of yourself, okay?'

'We'll have to see if I'm still around to eat the niangao you bring home next year.' He sounded morose, but a glimmer of determination in his eyes showed that he wasn't giving up just yet.

That night, Cousin called to thank me for visiting Uncle, and our conversation meandered to his health. She shared that the doctor had already warned about his worsening condition a few years back, so she was surprised that he'd managed to hold on this long. Even so, his eyesight had been deteriorating sharply, and he'd slowly lost his sense of taste.

'He's lost his sense of taste?'

'Yes.'

At that moment, everything clicked into place. I told Cousin the news.

Her mother—who is my uncle's first wife living in Guangzhou—passed away six months ago. On her deathbed, she'd asked her family not to tell my Uncle in Singapore about her death, to keep it from him until he himself passed on.

'So, please don't tell Uncle,' I said.

'Then, those niangao that you brought?'

'Aunt isn't around anymore, so of course her cakes are gone too. The niangao that I brought home this year aren't from her. I got them in Singapore, at the neighbourhood bakery.'

CULTURAL EXCHANGE

A group of American high school students would be visiting our school next month and joining us for lessons as part of a cultural exchange programme. When I told them about it during Chinese class, my students were very excited, proclaiming that they would be delighted to show the Americans around after school. I encouraged my students to write down the culturally significant places in Singapore worth taking them to.

The next day, a student named Jia Hanren showed me the list of places he would like to show the American students. The list was as follows:

1. Takashimaya
2. MacDonald
3. Boat Quay

I told him there weren't any places representative of his own culture on the list—how did he expect his visitors to get a sense of his culture? Furthermore, it was outrageous of him to hand me, a Mandarin Chinese teacher, a list of places written in English.

He took the list back and came to me again after some time. He had rewritten the list, and this time, it went like this:

1. GaoDaoWu
2. MaiDangLao
3. BoChuanMaTou

I was even more furious.

'And you call this Chinese?' I asked.

He gave me a piteous look. 'Sir, I don't know how to write the words in Chinese.'

I told him to consult the dictionary. Jia Hanren came back to me after an hour, and the final version looked like this, with each place written in Chinese characters:

1. 高岛屋
2. 麦当劳
3. 驳船码头

I gave him a pat on the back. 'Right, this is what I meant by your own culture.'

Before he went off, I asked, 'What are you going to do with your new friends at Boat Quay?'

He turned and flashed me a dazzling smile. 'We're going there for Mexican food.'

FIRST TIME HOME

A sense of excitement welled up inside him as he got off the bus with the other passengers. To his surprise, he hadn't overslept and missed his stop today.

As an assistant at a construction company, he had already dozed off countless times on his return journey from work. Endless upgrading projects had been demanding his attention: there were too many meeting reports to file; too many nights where sleep was a waking dream; too many winks to catch; too many missed stops as a result.

Day after day he sat on the bus, gazing out the window, his body jolting every now and then, keeping time with the stops and starts of the vehicle. One residential estate after another passed him by, each one exactly the same as the other. Without fail, he would let out a yawn in spite of himself.

He was embarrassed about his yawns at first but soon realised that the other commuters were yawning too, each to their own rhythm. Slowly, his eyelids grew heavy and he would fall into a deep slumber, in limbo between the soundless city and the choir of yawners.

Bewilderment gripped him every time he was roused from sleep. How many stops had he missed? The bus stops all looked identical—it seemed like any one of them could be his, and that he could get off at any one.

Time and again, he would spend ages figuring out exactly how far he'd gone on the bus route. He would then get off the bus, take another bus in the opposite direction, and try his best this time to stay awake.

But today, for the first time ever, he hadn't overshot. He'd woken up before his stop and couldn't contain his joy—it was as if he'd made a profit. Now he had extra time. He planned to have a good shower once he was home. Also, he would finally be able to catch the 7 p.m. sitcom that he always missed.

He set off from the bus stop and walked through the usual multi-storey car park. As always, a few female domestic helpers were waiting around the void decks of the HDB blocks for their employers' children to come home from school. Some people were holding a funeral. He was too exhausted and didn't give any of them a second glance.

As always, he pushed open the flap of his slot letterbox upon reaching his high-rise. There was nothing inside. Someone else in the family must have collected the letters. He glanced over the huge pile of junk mail lying in front of the rows and rows of metal letterboxes—flyers and ads that had been sent over and over for a good many years. Even so, the senders still tried their luck with the block's residents.

He squeezed into the usual lift. The people in the lift, packed like sardines in a mechanical box, all had the same blank expression as him, their eyes like those of dead fish. *Too tired,* he concluded. *Everyone's too tired.* He noticed that the flashing light in the lift, which had broken for ages, had finally been repaired.

After getting out of the lift, he passed his neighbours' flats. Their few potted plants looked exactly the same: all freshly watered, though one did seem new. He kicked away the slippers strewn all over the corridor as he walked, just like he always did.

The door to his flat was ajar, as usual. His children were at his neighbour's place again. Once in the living room, he threw his briefcase onto the sofa and a whiff of home-cooked food wafted out from the kitchen into his nose. His wife had been putting in extra hours at the office every night, coming home even later than him, so his mother-in-law had to do the cooking. The children must have taken the opportunity to sneak out to their neighbour's place while she was making dinner.

'I'm back,' he announced feebly in the direction of the kitchen. No response. There was only the sound of someone chopping vegetables on the chopping board. His mother-in-law's tinnitus was getting worse.

His fatigued body succumbed to the welcoming sofa, as his hand reached for the TV remote control on the coffee table. The evening news came on. It featured the usual newscaster with the usual expression, droning on at the usual pace, no surprises at all. The government's latest measure was announced. The other news items were neither good nor bad. Didn't he hear about that newly enacted measure last year, he thought to himself. Or was it last month? And this piece of news that he was watching now, hadn't it been reported last week? He was suddenly riddled with doubt, a sense of unease creeping up on him, making him wonder if he'd accidentally switched on the video tape recorder. He checked, but no: it was indeed today's news.

He was going to take a shower but had a hard time keeping his eyes open. He started to nod off when, suddenly, he missed his stop again! He sat up immediately. He caught sight of two children and an old woman sitting at the dining table having dinner in silence. They looked very much like his children and mother-in-law, except they weren't.

Who were they? How dare they barge into his place without his permission? He wanted to reproach them for their audacity but became aware that something was amiss with his flat—it looked somewhat different. But what was different? He could not put a finger on it. It then dawned on him that, alas, he was the intruder. This wasn't his home. It certainly looked like his. In fact, a bit too much.

He felt a sadness billowing within. Not because he had returned to someone else's home, but because no one in this flat had noticed him, an intruder, even though he had been in their flat for some time now. They are so alike, he thought to himself. Perhaps, their family member and he looked so alike that they had accepted his presence without question. In the end, his surging sadness didn't even spill over into a single tear. He left the flat quietly. By this time, the sky outside had already darkened.

In the dim light of dusk, he couldn't figure out where he was.

The high-rises surrounding the one where he stood all looked the same. He began to suspect that he'd got off at the wrong stop after all, and this housing estate was, in fact, not his.

This was the first time that he, as the nth citizen living an impeccable life in this immaculate city, going home to the nth meticulously-planned residential estate for the nth time, was lost in a myriad of units aglow with bright, beaming lights—none of which was his. He couldn't find his way home.

LU XUN AND THE JUJUBE TREES

Lu Xun:

From my backyard, I can see two trees beyond the wall. One is a jujube tree, the other one is also a jujube tree. There is no difference between Jujube One and Jujube Two. Even if they swap places, they are still jujube trees.

Jujube Trees:

In front of us, we can see two writers writing at their desks behind the window. One is Lu Xun, the other one is also Lu Xun. There is no difference between Lu Xun One and Lu Xun Two. Even if they swap places, they are still Lu Xun clones.

STREET SCENES

Street Scene 1:

She was seventeen that year. A big fan of romance novels. Sitting all alone in a cafe, poring over her sad novel one afternoon. In the story, the male protagonist stopped at the street corner, turned his head and took a glance at the female protagonist before he walked off, nary a care in the world. The female protagonist held back her tears, refusing to let them flow. She stood rooted to the spot, windblown, gazing at the back of the male protagonist disappearing into the distance.

On the street outside the cafe, a couple appeared to be tangled up with each other in a tussle as a huge crowd of onlookers gathered. Two waiters struck up a conversation, commenting on how the man should not have two-timed the woman. It was just his luck to have run into the woman he'd ditched on this fine day.

Through the window, she saw the woman's hair turn wild and unsightly from the wrangle. Half her body lay flat on the ground, her arms wrapped around the man's legs in a tight grip. The woman, who looked to be in her early thirties, had tears and snot smeared all over her face, and to top it all off, an uncouth black mole.

The seventeen year old, repulsed by the scene, shook her head and went back to reading her book. As she flipped the pages, a pretty red mole on the back of her hand came into view.

The fine aroma of coffee filled her seventeenth year.

Street Scene 2:

She was forty-five that year. Starting a decade ago, she had planted herself firmly in the small flower shop that she had nurtured with her own hands. She grew with the shop like a mythical blossoming flower, exuding an intoxicating scent now that she was in full bloom. She had a quiet elegance about her, her smile especially so. A lot of women loved to buy flowers from her and would stay on in the shop for a chat. It wasn't just the women who came; many middle-aged bachelors looked for excuses to patronise her shop too, chatting her up on the pretence of buying flowers. Some would come in to share a joke, whereas others would bring along a poem that they had written for her. She was the only flower in the shop that could never be enticed away, imbued with an easy confidence, rooted in grace. Never once did she droop like a wilting flower.

One afternoon, two ladies were in the shop chatting with her. Outside the glass door, a big crowd gathered on the street, watching a couple tangled up with each other in a tussle. One of the ladies went to find out what was going on, then came back to report that the man had apparently ditched the woman without a word. It was fortuitous that the scorned woman ran into the man today. To show she wasn't going to take it lying down, she refused to let him go.

The flower-shop owner looked through the glass door and saw a woman in her early thirties. Her hair was wild and unsightly, her face streaked with tears and snot. She was rolling on the ground, her arms wrapped tightly around the man's legs.

'Oh my god, there's blood on the back of her hand!' one of the ladies exclaimed.

The other lady chimed in. 'Gosh no, that's just a big, ugly red mole.'

The florist lowered her head, pointing at the roses that she had newly arranged. She asked the two ladies if they could give her some feedback. With that, their attention returned to the ageless roses.

Among the many flowers in the shop, the florist's side profile stood out. On her face, a sensuous black mole bobbed into view.

HOUSE

Year 2041

The ivory urn was awfully heavy to carry home. With a ton of care, he put the urn into the tallest cabinet in the study and closed the cabinet door.

He spoke in measured tones.

'Pa, I must say you really got foresight. Population's ageing, not many young, strong people left in this city, housing market crashed. But then, you know, among all the properties you've left me, the value of this one shot up due to market speculation. After I sealed the deal today, the agent and buyer kept thanking me. They kept praising you for your sharp judgment that year.'

He started up the computer. He has to re-watch the news clip from thirty years back, the one that his late father had played over and over again when he was alive.

Year 2001

Standing in front of the camera, he looked smug. In fact, the expression on his face was positively conceited because he'd been at the head of the line. The reporter from the TV station asked what he had to say about being the first batch of buyers to snap up the developer's ingenious idea: freehold grids that, although pricey, could be resold to anyone any time, including non-citizens.

He spoke in measured tones.

'I think this is a very good investment. They're going to exhume the graves in the Choa Chu Kang Cemetery soon, right? The grids here will sell like hot cakes when that happens. In Singapore, it's good to invest in the houses of the living, but it's even more important to beat the rest and invest in the houses of the dead.'

The camera was focused on him, and what lay behind him: the modern, beautifully furnished, so-called 'houses'. Most of the houses were empty, though some cremation urns, ivory in colour, had settled comfortably in a few of these houses. Then again, it might just be a temporary stay before they had to move again.

IT'S HISTORY ANYWAY

After his death, the poet woke up one day in 2084 to find his name listed in *Wenxue Shi*, a book about the History of Literature. He was elated beyond words. But his joy soured when he started to read his own biography, which went:

So-and-so, author. Born in 1964 in an unknown place. School unknown. Known for some literary style.

The poet went to look for the editor of *Wenxue Shi*. The editor was very polite, telling him the book was the latest edition and the previous one had been published twenty years ago. As most of the information in the previous edition was already outdated, they'd had to revise it and publish a new one.

The poet took the previous edition from the editor's hands. He flipped through the book and finally found his biography:

So-and-so, author. Born somewhere near New Port in 1964. Studied in Chong Mei Secondary School. Known for his poetry and has one poetry collection to his name.

The poet reproached the editor, demanding to know why his personal history had been falsified. He'd been born and raised in the Old Port, and his alma mater was Chong Zhen Secondary School. The poetry collection was titled *Children Who Grew Up Drinking the Old Port's Water*—why was that missing from his biography?

The editor, with much cordiality, told him that the names 'Old Port' and 'Chong Zhen Secondary School' had become obsolete two decades ago. The Old Port had already been upgraded and become the New Port; likewise, Chong Zhen Secondary School had changed its name to Chong Mei Secondary School. As for the name of the poetry collection, what is the point of mentioning the water of the Old Port when no one knew what 'Old Port' was anymore?

The poet pushed on with his questions. 'Okay, fine. Tell me why there're so many "unknowns" in this newest edition, then?'

'Well, it's because the New Port and Chong Mei Secondary School are now gone too. They've merged with other neighbourhoods and schools to become something else.'

The poet asked his final question. 'Why have you changed "poetry" to "some literary style" then?'

'Nobody uses "poetry" anymore. I haven't heard anyone mention the word in ten years. There's no such word in the latest Chinese writing software either.'

The dead poet was so incensed that, like an ignited rocket, he shot back to life.

Now, living in the year 2002, he's decided that he's going to live life to the fullest. He'll focus on living a good life. Might as well, since it's 'si' anyway—whatever happens, he's dead.

PUBIC HAIR

The door to the Abbess's office was slightly ajar. One of the nuns who'd recently arrived for duty at the convent had been summoned to the office. So rattled was she that she'd left the door unlatched when entering the room.

Through the crack in the door, the nun could be seen standing, her straight back in full view, hiding the Abbess from sight.

The door swayed slightly when the wind blew, and the sound of the Abbess's voice floated out through the door.

'Personal…clean…must every morning clean sheets on bed… can't be excused even one hair… shame…unclean…bad sheets… shame…'

The wind blew across the hall, backyard, kitchen, stairway and garden. Whispers drifted across the air like a susurration of the wind. Shocked faces blushed deep red one after another, like pollen disseminated by the wind's breath. In the end, even the old nun in the meditation room, who never cared for gossip, heard.

She knit her brows, her emotions a turbulent sea.

'What? Who has a man's hair of shame on her white bed sheet?'

FORTUNE AND BLISS

Fortune

It has been said that the people who discovered them did not react with shock or pity, but envy.

He and she were lying side by side on the bed in the motel—a picture of serenity. On the bedside table were a bottle of red wine and two wine glasses, the glasses still bearing remnants of their inebriation.

They were dressed to the nines, as if they'd been holding some kind of happiness ceremony to celebrate their fortune and bliss. Their composure divulged the bliss within.

The doctor who pumped their stomachs revealed that if they'd been discovered an hour later they would never have woken up.

Following that incident, her father finally agreed to let her leave the small town with the man. Everyone who saw them off beamed proudly at having witnessed the ending of such a fairytale. He, who was born with a limp, hobbled away, taking with him the daughter of the wealthiest and most distinguished man in town.

From then on, the smile on their faces—when they'd been found lying in bed, eyes tightly shut—became the sort of bliss that young people sought.

Bliss

It has been said that the people who discovered them did not react with shock or pity, but envy.

Almost everyone living on that street was already there before the police arrived. Each one of them appeared to be very calm, as if they were attending some kind of happiness ceremony. The owner of the flower shop said that they had passed by that morning, and that the man had bought the woman a rose. The florist had teased him about it, saying that it wasn't Monday, the day that he usually bought her flowers, and asked if he'd got the day wrong. The couple had smiled. She'd then asked him to buy a rose for Grandma Zhang too, the widow who lived alone down the street.

The guy working at the pharmacy told the police that, just the day before, they'd been at the pharmacy buying sleeping pills for two. While they'd waited for their pills, they'd begun discussing the plot of a novel that they'd just finished.

Their children and grandchildren all came back for the funeral despite living in various corners of the world. None of the children were rueful since their parents had led long, happy, healthy lives. Their parents had seldom been sick and preferred to live on their own, so each child used to take turns hosting them at their homes in different seasons.

Their youngest daughter took down the family photo on the wall. The picture was taken last year when the family had gathered to celebrate their sixtieth wedding anniversary. One of the guests had asked Ma if she'd had any regrets in her life, and she'd replied with a no. Only, she was afraid of death, so it would be better if Pa passed away first. Pa, with a smile, had said that Ma wasn't afraid of death, but rather of him being lonely if she were gone.

The youngest son took the two wine glasses as a keepsake. The neighbours down the street said they'd found them on the bed dressed to the nines, with a bottle of red wine and two wine glasses on the bedside table, the glasses still bearing remnants of their inebriation.

The eldest son took his father's crutch.

'For over fifty years, this crutch has been a part of Ma and Pa's two-person family. It's going to be so lonely now that Ma and Pa are gone.'

The eldest daughter took nothing. Before she left, she went to the only park in the small town and sat on the bench for a while. As she marvelled at the soft shades of salmon pink and apricot orange diffusing across the twilight sky, she imagined her Pa and Ma taking their walk at dusk every evening: singing songs, chatting with the children and feeding the birds. Even though he and she had visited many places all over the world, they still adored this small town with all their heart. After all, it was this town that had welcomed them sixty years ago with open arms.

The twilight was so beautiful. The eldest daughter ruminated on what the neighbours had said about Pa and Ma lying side by side on the bed, their eyes tightly shut, a smile on their faces. It must have been such a beautiful smile.

DISCLAIMER

Upon arrival, I see a sign not too far in the distance. I walk closer and the word *DISCLAIMER* comes into view. I take out my multilingual dictionary and look up the word. It's apparently *a statement that denies something, or anything related.*

There are eight regulations written under the heading *DISCLAIMER*:

1. Anyone who chooses to live here must take full responsibility
2. Anyone who was born here, whether voluntary or otherwise, with a single parent or parents who may not want to be responsible for their birth, must take full responsibility
3. Anyone who flies in the sky and gets struck by a missile must take full responsibility
4. Anyone who swims in the sea and has their skin corroded by chemicals must take full responsibility
5. Anyone who walks on Earth and steps on landmines leftover from the nth World War must take full responsibility
6. Anyone who contracts AIDS, regardless of whether they believe in love or not, must take full responsibility
7. Anyone, whether a passerby or visitor, appalled by the acts of their own kind destroying each other must take full responsibility
8. Anyone who has not read this warning and suffers any loss as a result must take full responsibility

The Undersigned,
Earth's Management

I take out the *Lonely Universe Independent Travel Guide* from my backpack and proceed to read the entry on Earth.

A rather small and troublesome place. During its heyday when it had not been misused, its environment was decent. Now, it has been ruined by visitors who decided to stay on for generations, adamantly refusing to budge. The place is a consequence of globalization. A day trip is tolerable but no longer than that. During your time there, avoid speaking to creatures called 'humans'.

After reading the entry, I'm of two minds, wondering if I should stop over after all, when a creature wearing a mask walks slowly towards me. From where I am, I can see it holding an inferior combat toy. Feeling all kinds of disappointment, I head back to the spaceship and set course for Mercury instead.

THREE PERCENT

A dream.

Not long after the Goods and Services Tax Act is passed, the Audit Committee summons three authors for simultaneous questioning.

Author A stands accused of using numerous ellipses in his work when the Goods and Services Tax Act came into force. Not only that, he has cut his long paragraphs short, writing much fewer words than before, but for the same amount of money. On the surface, he hasn't received more money for his writing compared to before, but any reader who buys his books now gets less from them.

Author A counters: *[150 words deleted]*. The auditor responds: *[three words deleted]*. Despondent and helpless, Author A walks away.

Author B increased his writing fee to cover the cost increase and thus stands accused of using the GST hike to his advantage. His reasoning is, the paper and pen that he uses to write are technically goods, and so are the cafe where he writes—they are his sources of inspiration. Therefore, he needs to increase his fee to cover the cost of those things. However, his writing is a work of art. It is classified as Literature, a lofty art that enriches the mind and soul. Therefore it cannot be considered a good or service. Writing is a manifestation of the author's conscience, a moral obligation that he, as an artist living in a capitalistic society, has to the people.

Author B retorts: *[300 words deleted]*. The auditor replies: *[three words deleted]*. Filled with resentment and hurt, Author B walks away.

Author C beats the auditor to the punch, declaring that he has always filed a clear and detailed tax report. Since his annual earnings are over a million dollars, he has voluntarily increased his writing fee by three percent. He has not only helped the nation gain more tax revenue in an honest manner, but, as one of many authors trapped in a declining industry, he has also helped authors in general regain some dignity. Is there anything wrong with that?

The auditor panics: *[27 words deleted, including exclamation marks and ellipses].* Author C walks away with his head held high and his chest puffed up.

After a few days, various media outlets hound Author C for interviews. Public opinion is brutal, but the most hurtful part of it all is the disbelief: how can an author be making so much money?

After a while, the media storm dies down. Some say that the author actually passed on long ago, and that the person questioned was actually the author's twin brother—a teacher/journalist/editor/ad-agency copywriter/broadcast writer. His annual income does in fact exceed a million dollars but only due to his investment in stocks.

The three percent continues.

(Note: If the reader suspects that short sentences are being used to replace long paragraphs just so the author can do less work and still ask for the same writing fee, please feel free to delete the first paragraph.)

FINS

During dinner, my son always loves to talk about what's happening at school.

'There's this boy in my class. His father came to pass him his lunchbox today and everyone was shocked.'

I kept quiet, duly focused on gulping down my rice. My wife, on the other hand, was her usual determined-to-acknowledge-whatever-my-son-says self, so she encouraged him to go on.

'His father didn't have a single fin on him!' exclaimed our son.

'There's nothing strange about that. Some people in our society aren't fully evolved yet.' As my wife spoke, the pretty fins on her throat rose and fell like undulating waves. Ah, she's such a picture of grace.

'But everyone in class has fins on them, except that boy. His fins are so teeny-weeny that he looks super weird. Now that we've met his father, we finally know why.'

I didn't cut in on their conversation. Dinner was really good today.

'His father was speaking to him in a language that we didn't understand. But actually, the boy didn't look happy about speaking that language. At least, not in front of all of us.'

'It's Wala-Wala,' my wife told him.

'Wala-Wala?'

'The language that people used to speak before we evolved to speaking Eli-Eli. Not many people can speak Wala-Wala these days.'

'Oh, I remember. When Grandpa and Grandma were alive, they spoke that language! I was still small then. So, the language they used to speak was the one the boy's father spoke this afternoon! Now I get it. Grandma and Grandpa didn't have fins. Mum and Dad, you can't speak Wala-Wala, so you both have fins. And since you two have fins, I was born with them too!'

I'd finally finished my food, so I decided to chime in.

'Our fins only started to grow when we were older. Yours are different. You were born with those fins, so you have to cherish your good genes.'

As I spoke, I could feel my fins rising and falling gracefully.

I have the good habit of rinsing my mouth after meals. As I started towards the bathroom, I overheard my wife and son talking.

'I suppose your classmate was very embarrassed?'

'Before school dismissed today, he was moved to the lousiest class. The class is full of students with misshapen fins.'

I went into the bathroom and closed the door. I relieved myself, brushed my teeth, rinsed my mouth, and looked at myself in the mirror. I detached my fins. I could never let my wife know my long-kept secret.

Only the people who have completely forgotten how to speak Wala-Wala can grow fins. My wife made a pact with me: for the sake of our children, we had to let our fins grow. We tried very hard to convince ourselves and other people that we didn't speak or understand Wala-Wala. That we spoke Eli-Eli, even in our dreams.

My wife was my role model. So when we made love, or when I fell into a contemplative mood, the Eli-Eli language began to come naturally to me. However, in my dreams, I still spoke Wala-Wala, like I did as a kid.

As my wife became more charged with determination to succeed and her fins started to grow, I secretly bought a pair of fake fins. The shop owner who specialised in selling fake fins told me that, in actual fact, many people were walking around with false fins that rose and fell as if they were real.

'Half those fins are fake,' he said. 'The workmanship is so meticulous, you simply can't tell the difference.'

I reattached the fins to my throat and looked in the mirror. 'Son, you're lucky you've got your mother's genes,' I muttered. 'Our whole family lives and breathes as one. At long last, with your birth, we have successfully evolved.

QUEUE

'Hello Sir, what would you like to eat?'

The lady running the economy rice stall looks a harried sight as she tends to all the students queuing to buy food after school. When she raises her head and sees the teacher, she waves, motioning him to move forward to the head of the queue.

The voice is a familiar one. He's heard it untold times, starting many, many years ago, and now he knows it well. Back in those days, after history class ended, the teacher would always instruct him to buy his lunch and bring it to him in the staff room. Whenever he went to the rice stall, the woman would immediately spot him in the endless queue. She would then call him forward and give him priority over everyone else.

'What would the teacher like to eat?'

In those days, it was an honour to help teachers buy their food. Stuck in the queue for his own meals, he would fantasise about the day he would finally become a teacher.

As he opens his mouth to answer the woman, he suddenly remembers Old Chen's expression as he packed the things on his desk into a large cardboard box. Old Chen's indignation rings loud and clear in his ears.

'I can't take this lying down!'

He tried to persuade Old Chen to stay on, but Old Chen refused. It was just yesterday when it all happened. Old Chen went to the canteen to buy his lunch and the noodle stall owner, as usual, gave him priority over the rest of the queue. Afterwards, the principal had summoned Old Chen to his office. A student had made a complaint about some teacher not queuing up to buy food.

The principal had told the student that he should have been brave and called out said teacher right there and then, in the queue. He showed the student a faculty group photo on his wall and made the student point out which teacher it was. Then Old Chen was called in and given a warning.

He can't forget how Old Mr. Chen marched out of the staff room carrying the enormous cardboard box. The sight of Old Chen disappearing into the distance reminded him of his old history teacher, though Old Chen's back wasn't as straight and strong…

It's been fifteen years since he started teaching, and he has never asked a student to buy him lunch. He has been exceptionally cautious. So much so that he even drills this school rule into his head: never ask students to clean the blackboard. He doesn't want to step on anyone's toes.

'Sir, what do you want to eat?' The stall owner ignores the queue once more, stopping her flurried activity and, again, motioning him to come to the front.

For the first time in fifteen years, he doesn't walk to the head of the queue. Instead, he remains in the never-ending line of people and, with a tinge of embarrassment, says: 'It's okay. I can, uh, queue and wait for my turn.'

BUT MEMORIES, THEY LINGER IN MY MIND

Ah Mei

Time flies and never returns

I've known this song since I was ten. Everyone in the town knew it like the back of their hand. It was so popular.

But memories, they linger in my mind

Sister Qin sang this song especially well; it was heaven to my ears. She didn't sing it in front of just anybody, only Ah Xiong and I were lucky enough to hear her crooning softly as she did the household chores. As a matter of fact, it was from her that Ah Xiong and I learnt how to sing this song.

We were childhood sweethearts

Ah Xiong, my next-door neighbour, was two years older than me. We grew up together. Every day, we would go to school together and find ways to amuse ourselves. We loved playing in the sand when we were small, often getting ourselves very dirty. We were so terrified of getting a scolding from the adults that we would enter the house through the back door before anyone had a chance to tell us off. Sister Qin would often bathe us in secret so that the two of us would be clean and fresh, together.

We were childhood playmates, day and night

Ah Xiong's parents and mine were always busy running their businesses, but he and I had each other, day and night. Sometimes, when Ah Xiong was too tired from playing, he would sleep over at my place. I have to say, he wasn't the most peaceful sleeper, and would often kick me out of bed. At times, I'd get so angry that I'd chase him out into the living room. He would sleep there till sunrise, then make his way home on his own.

Flowers blush once more in the spring wind

Those were the days when I thought Ah Xiong and I would stay that way forever. I even told Ah Xiong, 'I want to marry you when I grow up.' One time, I saw him enter my house with a flower in his hand and found it lying on my table when I got home. For the first time ever, I felt myself flush with happiness.

You are once more a year older too

I was twelve when Ah Xiong and I suddenly grew apart. It's still as clear as day in my memory. Mama told me it was natural for boys to want to play with other boys when they were older. But I was terribly sad all the same. That year, Sister Qin went missing and Ah Xiong wouldn't speak to me anymore.

Your heart's changing course, like time gone and lost

Today, I went out to celebrate my thirtieth birthday alone. And, to my surprise, I ran into Ah Xiong on the street. He left our town when I was eighteen. It's been so many years since I last saw him and now he has an air of maturity about him. The woman next to him looked familiar, but I wasn't sure where I had seen her before.

Only in my dreams I hold you close

I return to the apartment where I live by myself. Night has fallen, but I can't sleep. It's as if I'm twelve again, back in my small town, awash in the same feelings I had one night long ago. That night, when I was sleeping, Ah Xiong gave me a hug so light. And, very softly, he let go. Was it a dream, or did it really happen? I will never know.

Ah Xiong

Time flies and never returns

I've known this song since I was twelve. Everyone in the town knew it like the back of their hand. It was that popular.

But memories, they linger in my mind

Sister Qin, who was older than me by four years, was the most mesmerizing when she sang this song. Both Ah Mei and I called her Sister Qin as kids. My Ma kept saying even though it was okay for me to call her Sister Qin, Ah Mei really should be calling her 'sister-in-law'. Apparently, Ah Mei's Mama had an older brother who died young, and Sister Qin was his child bride. I remember asking Ma what a child bride was, but she said I'd find out when I was older.

We were childhood sweethearts

Ah Mei, my next-door neighbour, was two years younger than me. We grew up together. We went to school together, we played together. When we were small, Sister Qin would often give us baths together. I can't remember exactly when I started to enjoy having Sister Qin bathe me. In fact, I would deliberately play in the sand with Ah Mei so we would get dirty and Sister Qin would have to give us a bath.

We were childhood playmates, day and night

One time, when Sister Qin was giving me a bath, she started singing this song. I didn't know what came over her, but a rosy red bloomed in her cheeks when she came to this line: 'we were childhood playmates, day and night.' A smile, like a soft flower petal, unfurled on her face.

When I was sleeping over at Ah Mei's place one night, she chased me out of her bed and I had to sleep in the living room. Around midnight, I woke up to pee and caught Sister Qin walking furtively back to her bedroom through the back door. There was that same mysterious smile on her face—the smile that looked exactly like the one I'd seen when she was giving me a bath.

Flowers blush once more in the spring wind

In spring that year, the wildflowers along the road were in full bloom. I had no idea why, but I wanted to give Sister Qin a flower so badly. I picked one, sneaked into Ah Mei's house and put the flower on the table in Sister Qin's room. As I was leaving, I saw Sister Qin entering the house through the front door. My face suddenly blushed bright scarlet, so I took to my heels and stole out of the house through the back. At the time, I thought I would be brave enough to tell Sister Qin one day, 'I want to marry you when I grow up.'

You are once more a year older too

The memories are so clear in my mind. I was fourteen when Sister Qin and I suddenly grew apart. She ignored me when I went to speak to her but kept singing that song instead. I slept over at Ah Mei's place again one night and, once more, she chased me out into the living room. I was awoken by some sounds at midnight, and saw Sister Qin slipping out of the house through the back door. I followed close behind.

Your heart's changing course, like time gone and lost

I will always remember how Sister Qin looked at me that night. In the moonlight, I could see her with someone under a big tree. The glow from the moon revealed it was Brother Chang, who lived at the end of the alley. He was older than Sister Qin by two years. I noticed Sister Qin was carrying a cloth bundle and Brother Chang had a box with him. They saw me. It didn't take me long to figure out what they wanted to do. If I had cried out, they wouldn't be able to leave. But I didn't. Sister Qin looked at me coolly, and the three of us stood there in silence. After standing there for what felt like a very long time, Sister Qin gently took Brother Chang's hand. Both of them, hand in hand, slowly walked away by the light of the moon. They never came back.

Only in my dreams, I hold you close

I call out for Sister Qin in my sleep tonight, holding Lisa in my arms. I don't think Lisa realises—she's drifting between the dream world and the waking world. Even if she does hear me, she won't know it's because I ran into Ah Mei today. I'm not sure if Ah Mei noticed that Lisa looked a bit like Sister Qin. I'd always hoped that Ah Mei would never find out about what happened that year, that night.

Sister Qin and Brother Chang were gone, leaving me to find my way home myself like a lost soul. I ended up in Ah Mei's house, where I went straight into Sister Qin's room. It was true—she wasn't there anymore. Ah Mei was sound asleep when I walked into her room. I hugged her lightly, and imagined that I was hugging Sister Qin. After that, I walked back home and never visited Ah Mei again.

FLY THE COOP

The Centres for Disease Control and Prevention in the United States report that cholera is slowly spreading among the Rwandan refugees who have fled to Zaire. The number of deaths is on the rise.

'What's wrong with you?'

'I can't do this. I just can't crawl anymore.'

'Hey, chin up. Our whole tribe's just as desperate as you.'

'Just leave me be…'

At present, more than 1.2 million refugees are swarming towards Goma in Zaire. As the cholera spreads like wildfire, the refugees find themselves in grave need of food and clean water.

'I'm so tired. I feel so weak. Where else do we need to go?'

'I don't know either, but our hometown's in deep shit. It's in our best interests to follow the others and get as far away as we can.'

'I don't think I can keep up. Can't believe I'm going to die a lonely death in a foreign land. You should go on your merry way.'

'Are you dumb? If you want to die, we'll die together.'

The experts have predicted infected cases to be as high as fifty thousand, and that half those cases are unlikely to pull through.

'Is this the refugee camp or a mass grave? Oh my, so many dead bodies here, lying side by side in neat little rows! Are they our brothers from our tribe?'

'Strange. These corpses are all huddled together. They look like us and yet not. I mean, on closer look, they seem to be shadows on the floor…'

'Oh no! What happened? What's that smell? See that huge commotion over there? Are the enemies here? Wait, is it a tornado? They're all coming back here! Hey you, there's no space. Stop crowding in on me, you fool! Don't trample me!'

'Where are you? I can't see you. Help!'

*

The swarm of ants were in the middle of a big move, scurrying frenetically across last night's newspaper. They were crawling over a news article about the Rwandan refugees when she discovered them. She hated ants with a vengeance, and immediately grabbed and sprayed them with insecticide without mercy.

Just as she was about to sweep away the many dead bodies lying limp and lifeless on the floor, she came across the news about the cholera outbreak among the Rwandan refugees. The photos from Reuters showed the famished refugees strewn across the ravaged land—a devastating sight that wrenched the heart. In the photos, a man carried his dead wife to a mass grave, putting her dead body with other corpses neatly arranged side by side.

Her eyes reddened. She couldn't bear to continue reading, so she put the newspaper back where it was supposed to be and swiftly swept up the countless ant corpses covering the floor.

THE DEFINING MOMENT

The male lead stands on stage and delivers his famous monologue—one that will determine whether he'll receive rounds of deafening applause to bask in. It's his defining moment.

Round after round of applause reverberates across the theatre. Without a doubt, the male lead has once again captivated the audience's hearts. He's played this scene so many times by now that his acting prowess is evident.

The play itself is called *The Defining Moment*, and it's the theatre troupe's sell-out show. There's a classic scene that comes at the end. Here, the male lead has almost given up hope, which is also the precise moment the female lead steps in. Even though she appears only for a few minutes, she is given her own ballad to sing and a few stirring lines—just the right combination she needs to slip into the audience's hearts.

In just three minutes, the female lead will make her entrance. She stands in the wings without a word, just as she's done for the past twenty years. Out of habit, she quickly runs through the song in her heart, as she always does for every performance.

Xiao Zhang, the prompter, walks past and, as usual, gives her a smile. Or perhaps, 'as usual' isn't the right word tonight. It's her last night with the troupe. According to the rules of the group, no one—whether a leading actor or minor character—is allowed to perform once they turn forty. The rule applies for everyone in the troupe—there is no exception.

Many of the people who have come to watch tonight have been staunch supporters of the troupe for a good many years. On this particular night, they've come especially to support the female lead—this is, after all, her last night performing for the troupe.

In just two minutes, the female lead will have her defining moment. This moment will determine her fate: whether she goes out in a blaze of glory or not.

Old Lin, the assistant director, walks past and gives her a pat on the shoulder. She's used to it. Many years ago, that little pat meant, *Everything depends on the next minute.* But tonight it means, *Everything depends on tonight.*

Finally, with only one minute to go, the stage lighting changes and the music intensifies, setting the scene for the female lead. She takes a deep breath. *Everything depends on tonight.*

Thirty seconds left now. The stage curtains part. She sees the female lead and her assistant approach and stop. Even though she's standing beside them, they don't even spare her a glance. In just ten seconds, the lead will have to step onstage. This is the defining moment. As on every other performance night, the female lead's assistant, with utmost deference, gives her a look that says it's time.

She understands that look. It's one that she's replayed over and over in her mind. Actually, when the curtains parted, she already knew the moment that belonged to her, her last defining moment, was over.

The female lead steps out and takes her place centre stage. She launches into that classic song. The audience responds with thunderous applause, so loud it feels like it's shaking the heavens.

Without a sound, she stays put and admires the female lead from where she stands. She feels like she's looking at herself on the stage tonight. That it's not the female lead onstage, in the spotlight—it's her. She's singing the song that she's practised so hard, every single day—so hard that her heart can hum every word, hit every note without prompt.

It's not just once that Xiao Zhang has told her, 'To be honest, you sing the song with more feeling.'

She would reply with a smile. 'Too bad the audience doesn't have an opportunity to hear me sing.'

'You never know,' Old Lin has told her many times. 'If there's just one time when the female lead can't go onstage for whatever reason, you'll get your chance to sing in her place. I bet you'll be an instant hit.'

Yes. She had once thought that she needed 'just one time'.

The female lead stops singing. Together with the male lead, they bow to the audience's thunderous applause as the curtains fall. She's replayed this applause over and over in her mind from her spot in the wings. On this night, this very last night with the theatre troupe, she basks in the applause for the very last time.

Twenty years ago, the troupe director had made himself clear. He had signed on two actresses at one go: one was cast as the resident female lead, and the other as the permanent understudy. If there ever came a time where the female lead couldn't go onstage, the understudy would take her place immediately. That year, she was a twenty-year old actress, exactly the same age as the female lead who has now taken centre stage for the past twenty years.

The theatre empties. Without a word, she bids farewell to *The Defining Moment*. She returns to the dressing room, removes her makeup, and waits for Old Lin and the rest to treat her to supper for the last time.

DECLARATION

My girlfriend's parents have finally invited me over to their place for a meal. To start us off with a 'meet', as they say. It didn't come easy.

Thing is, my girlfriend's father belongs to the upper echelons of society, so one can imagine how difficult it is for the man in the street to meet someone of his stature, let alone visit him at his residence. Yet he's willing to meet me even during pandemic times, so I gather the gesture is a tacit approval of me as his future son-in-law.

Before the meeting, my girlfriend helps me mentally prepare for what's to come.

'My father's very stern. He's a man of few words.'

'No problem.'

'You might not be used to the ways of the butlers and servants.'

'No problem.'

'If anything awkward happens, please try to bear with it for my sake.'

'Well, anything for you. No problem at all.'

On the day of the meeting, I make an attempt to look more presentable. I'm fifteen minutes early when I arrive at the door of my girlfriend's mansion. The timing is perfect: not so early that it's more intrusive than polite, nor so late that I'll definitely be seen as downright rude.

The servant who answers the door keeps me waiting outside for some time. The butler comes out soon after and, very politely, gives me a form. 'I'm so sorry, but could you please fill in this health declaration form first? It's just the procedure here.'

At first, I find it a tad ridiculous. After some thought, it makes complete sense. My girlfriend's father isn't any John Doe, meaning that anyone who visits him will have to be of some status. What's more, he has to be cautious about strangers spreading viruses in his mansion.

The questions on the declaration form are very familiar; I see them everywhere these days. In fact, I've practically memorised them:

1. Have you been to any outbreak locations in the past 10 days?
2. Have you been in contact with any infected person or any person suspected of being infected?
3. Do you have flu or fever symptoms?

I answer no to all the questions and return the form. The butler takes a look and nods. He then gives me another form to fill in. I take a look and see it's a *Mental Health Declaration Form*.

The butler seems to notice my strange expression, so he lowers his voice: 'I hope you won't take this to heart. This is an honour. Only people who have the honour to visit Master have the chance to fill in this form.'

These are the questions on the form:

1. Have you been involved in any artistic or philosophical work in the past 10 years?
2. Have you let anyone into your heart or has anyone let you into their heart in the past 10 years?
3. Do you have symptoms that show an extravagant passion for life?

I look at the questions for a very long time and hand the form back to the butler.

'I'm so sorry, but you haven't filled in the form,' says the butler.

I smile. 'It isn't necessary. I've decided to isolate myself.'

LABEL

At long last, he thought, *I don't have a problem with labels anymore.*

When he was three, his father would put labels on everything in the house so he would be able to associate words with the correct objects: the table was labelled *table,* the door was labelled *door.* That way, he would pick up the words very quickly. Only the word *I* didn't work as expected. Even though he was labelled *I,* he could never see the word on himself, which meant that he never managed to learn how to write it. In the end, when he was changing one day, the label fell off.

When he was in Primary Five, there was one time he forgot to bring his completed homework to school. He told the teacher the truth, but the teacher put a label on his forehead that read: *I lied.* He was only allowed to remove it after school dismissal.

One time, during National Service, he had to take the old lady next door to the hospital, so he couldn't make it back to camp by the time he was supposed to return. In fact, he was spotted and apprehended on his way back. As punishment, he was locked up for a week. On his release, his commander insisted on putting a label on the front of his uniform that read *deserter.* He had no choice but to keep it there for a whole month.

Before he turned thirty, he became a famous author. Often, he would walk quietly into the bookshop and admire the various labels that the publisher had put on his books: *an avant-garde author; a literary figure ahead of his times; the people's spokesperson.*

After he turned forty, he was incarcerated. A regime change had rocked the country and the then leader felt that the author had smeared his image in his most notable work. All his books were burned except for one that was kept locked and barred from access in a secret storage place at the National Library. It was labelled *Banned Book.*

In his old age, he would sit at home and his family would play the same videotape for him to watch every day. His sight was failing, so he preferred to watch the same classic scene again and again: a video recording of the day he was released from jail, when he became the national news highlight. The newly elected president had personally welcomed him back into society and had even draped a sash of glory over his shoulder.

The words on the sash were too small to make out on the TV screen. He would ask his family every day if the word on the sash really read *hero*? Had he been labelled a *hero*? Every day, his family would reply yes. His worries were then put to rest, and he would turn around and look for the I that he'd lost when he was a child.

Now, he thought, *I don't have a problem with labels anymore.*

He was now a pile of ashes. His family had been respectful of his wishes and had granted them by cremating him. He didn't think there was anything left to label—he was a mere pile of ashes.

He revelled in this thought, finally free of all worries, when an executive from the columbarium walked over. The executive started putting numbered labels on the funerary urn niches, ordered according to the annual fee paid for each urn.

WINK

It's become a routine—how every day, at this hour, they lock eyes with each other.

Every day, at this hour, the person driving the car takes a short cut. He travels on this secluded road, past the front door of some politician's mansion, and reduces his speed as he approaches the speed bump.

Every day, during his afternoon shift, the person standing guard notices a red sports car driving past. The driver is always the same dashing man with long hair.

Every day, the one driving casually flicks a glance at the guard as he drives by, taking in his imposing presence; his upright posture; his square face; his short hair. A thought flits into his head: how long would I be able to stand like that in this treacherous heat? If I were in his place for even one minute, how fun would it be?

Every day, the one standing guard casts a glance at the driver. Having undergone strict training, he has to make sure he keeps a stern face at all times. His mind, though, is a flutter of thoughts: if only I could race down the road in a red sports car like him for just one minute. It would be such fun.

Every day, for one second, their eyes lock. Every day, for one second, both are unaware, or rather, pretend to be unaware, of how they have their eye on the other. Every day, for one second, the one driving the car has his fleeting thought, just as the one standing guard has his fleeting thought.

As the driver speeds past every day, he realises that he yearns to catch sight of the guard. When he was in secondary school, the National Police Cadet Corps rejected him because he was in poor physical shape. Seeing the guard turns him into the person in uniform: short hair, square face, straight posture. He wants to stop the car, but he can't—he's already passed the mansion.

The man standing guard finds the man driving the sports car occupying his thoughts more and more. He was born into a poor family. Once, when he was playing at his cousin's place, he accidentally broke a small red remote-control sports car. Afterwards, he was forbidden from going to his cousin's place. Seeing the speeding sports car turns him into the driver: long hair, tall, dashing looks. He wants to stop the car, but he can't—he has to maintain a stern expression.

The one driving begins to doubt himself: why is he so interested in a man? He even wants to—actually wants to!—wink at the guard with his left eye, like he would do to a woman he were interested in. A devil-may-care wink lasting a split second, so quick that he won't even have to admit to having winked. But the other person seems so stern, and he's such a macho man himself.

The one standing guard starts to wonder: is he attracted to the man driving the sports car? Impossible. He already has a girlfriend. Yet he actually wants to wink at the man driving the sports car with his left eye! Just a quick wink that a man flirting with a woman might revel in. He doesn't even have to admit to winking afterwards, not even if the other person sees it. But surely he does want the other person to see the wink? Isn't that what a wink is supposed to do? He really shouldn't be afraid. Even if the man does see it, he'll be incredulous.

It's probably very much like a person standing in front of a mirror, besieged by a longing to wink at himself but deeply afraid of being noticed by someone. He feels like an outsider stuck outside the mirror; an outsider that can never enter the mirror because of an invisible barrier. Is he also forbidden from winking at himself in the mirror if he ever wants to prove *I exist* and *I miss him*? The one driving the car mulls over this, the one standing guard mulls over this. Day after day, desire surges like the noon temperature, without a sound.

Today is like any other day. When the one driving passes the mansion, he manages to restrain himself. The one standing guard manages to restrain himself too. But then, in that split second, both catch the other person winking suggestively at him.

Am I imagining things? The car speeds past. One of them is in the car, the other is standing guard, but both are simultaneously taken aback and unsure.

The person on land sees the narcissus flower winking at him, but the narcissus flowering in the water sees the person on land winking. In that blink of an eye, could it have been misinterpreted either way?

The light refracted from the water and the light refracted from the mirror are equally blinding. The one driving and the one standing guard both squint in the sizzling heat.

ROLL CALL

12 May 2001

The news below broke in Singapore's Chinese paper *Lianhe Zaobao*:

From next year onwards, primary and secondary school students will be able to flash a smart card in front of a sensor at the school entrance. This will help relieve the school of heavy administrative duties—in this case, the daily roll call conducted by teachers. Instead, a computer will automatically record the student's name and their arrival time at school.

On the x day of x month in x year, a teacher is about to pass away

'Wang Guomin.'

'Here.'

Hmm. The kid's voice is turning more and more hoarse. Must be a puberty thing.

'Liu Xiaohua.'

'Here.'

He's mischievous and can be a handful, but every time I call his name during roll call, he shows such enthusiasm for class.

Lin Xiulan. Lin Xiulan. Lin…XIU…LAN.

Not here! Is she sick again? I'd better call her parents in the afternoon.

'Chen Enhui.'

'Here.'

Not only does Enhui look like her older sister, she sounds like her as well. I had Enyi last year. They sound so alike.

'Zhao Mingde.'

'Here.'

Mingde's essays have improved a lot recently. I should praise him in class during our next essay feedback session.

*

The school secretary, Miss Zhang, told the principal, 'Mr. Tan, one of Mr. Huang Yucai's relatives called this morning. They said he was all right last night, but failed to wake up this morning. It seems he has passed away. According to the family member, his heart stopped. But there was a smile on his face, as if he was dreaming of something lovely.'

On the x day of x month in x year, a sensor is about to break

01365489, a flash.
-------------------------------. 0650.
01896757, a flash.
-------------------------------. 0651.
01569874, a flash.
-------------------------------. 0658.
012896736, a flash.
-------------------------------. 0701.
02679882, a flash.
Flash.
One more flash.
-------------------------------.

The school secretary, Miss Zhang, told the principal, 'Mr. Tan, the smart card sensor at the school entrance was fine yesterday but suddenly broke down this morning. Seems it broke after a student yelled something at it.'
'What did he yell?'
'Here.'

THE RIGHT EAR

A friend texts me: *Can you answer the phone, please?*

I reply: *The ringtone on my handphone isn't working. I can only send and receive texts at the moment.*

The friend texts again: *There's something wrong with my ear.*

I reply: *Of course. An ear has always been a hear to you. You've never said it correctly.*

The friend texts: *I'm not joking. There's really something wrong with my ear. I woke up today and realised that one of my ears can't hear anything.*

The left one or the right?

Right.

Sounds great. You'll just have to cover your left ear in the future to shut out all the noise in this world.

I'm not joking. I'm at the hospital now. Anyway, talk to you later. It's my turn to see the doc.

My friend's quite the joker, which makes me kind of dubious about his texts. But if there's indeed a problem with his ear, then it's not going to bode well for him. He's a composer. It's going to be quite troublesome for a composer to be hard of hearing, even if it's just one ear that's affected. I mean, he's not Beethoven, is he?

I take off my earphones, feeling the serenity of my surroundings.

Believe it or not, I've been listening to music with earphones on for three consecutive days and nights. I've been staring at my computer and rushing a report. Other than eating bowls of instant noodles, going to the bathroom and catching a few winks, I've just been listening to music non-stop. My earphones seem to be a bit broken; the sound's not very good in the right side. But I can't concentrate on my work when there aren't earphones blasting music into my ears.

My friend texts me again: *Can you come to the hospital real quick? The doctor says my right ear has to be amputated today or my life will be in danger. If you visit me tomorrow, I won't be able to hear you speak at all. And even if I can, I won't hear in stereo anymore.*

Ok. I'll come visit tomorrow, then. Just to see where your right hear has hidden itself.

I'm NOT JOKING. Come visit me NOW. They're going to put me under anaesthesia in an hour.

Anaesthesia? Oh, I've been listening to that Anaesthesia song by Faye Wong for the past few days. I'm so hooked. I think I'm pretty much anaesthetised too.

My friend texts: *Go die.*

I don't go die like he suggests, but my handphone does. The battery's dead, so I start charging it. All of a sudden, I feel hungry. *Might head downstairs and get a burger,* I think.

The next-door auntie takes the same lift. She seems to be moving her lips. I want to take my earphones off so I can understand what she's saying, but she just smiles and closes her mouth again. Did I imagine it? I mean, she's never spoken to me before. When the lift reaches the ground floor, both of us leave the building and head in different directions, like two ears destined not to hear each other.

A lot of people look at me when I walk into the fast-food restaurant. City folk really have a way with this—they can look at you and look like they aren't really looking at you. Well, I've got my ways too. I respond with a look that seems to say I'm not looking at them but, actually, I am. I walk up to the counter and the lady moves her mouth politely. I can read from her lips that she's asking me what I'd like to order. I tell her I want a burger. She gestures for me to remove my earphones.

I remove my earphones and ask what her question is. It's very strange, but I still can't hear in stereo even after removing my earphones. She's a bit hesitant, and somewhat uneasy. 'Um sir, you didn't bring your right ear with you.'

I laugh and say, yeah, I left it at home to be charged. As I speak, I reach for my right ear and feel around. Shit. Where is it? Suddenly, I hear my phone ringing. My left ear says it's my landline. But of course. I mean, my handphone has died, and there's an answering machine at home. *Riiiiing…riiiiing…riiiiing.* I rush home to pick up my phone. Despite having brought only one ear with me I can hear the ringing loud and clear. The phone rings on: Riiiiing. Riiiiing. Riiiiing. I ask the people I pass: do you hear the ringing? They just look blankly at me. One of them even tries to show me how he can flap his ears.

Pathetic fool.

In the lift, the ringing from home becomes more and more distinct. *Ring. Riing. Riiing. RIIIIIIIIIIIIIING.*

'Do you hear that?'

I'm asking the auntie who took the lift down with me a while ago. She's bought her vegetables and is now in the same lift heading up. She looks as if she's about to open her mouth but stops. Seems she was just smiling.

'Go and die.'

Riiiiing. Riiiiing. Riiiiing. I walk out of the lift and think, *Did I actually just open my mouth and tell her to go die?*

I fumble for my keys and open the door. I rush to the answering machine but the ringing stops as soon as I pick up the receiver. Was it ringing? Or was it a hallucination? My ear, no wait, my handphone, starts to ring. It's working now that it's charged.

'Hello? Hello?' I say.

It's my friend. 'Didn't you say there's something wrong with your handphone's ringtone?'

'Then why are you calling?'

'I'm just calling to say you're a damn lousy friend. If I ever lose both my *hears*, you'll be the last person I rely on.'

'Can you stop bothering me already? I'm looking for my *hear* now. Damn it. I mean, *ear.*'

My friend laughs. 'So you've got a problem with your *hear* now, you say?'

Furious, I hang up the phone. Where's my ear? Where the hell's my ear? I look all over the living room, bedroom, and even check the toilet bowl in the bathroom. There's no ear to be found. One of my ears has really hidden itself. One of my *hears* is gone.

The world can come to a standstill for all I care, but I have to rush to finish this report. I switch on the computer and there onscreen, my right ear appears, alone and forlorn.

I even hear it sobbing softly.

OPERATION

1.

Everything was dazzlingly white when he woke up. Strong white light, white room, white curtains, men and women in white gowns.

White is the colour of hygiene.

He smiled and asked, 'Has it been removed?'

They smiled back saying of course it had. The surgery was an absolute success. He lifted the white sheet. What?! His manhood was gone.

'Is this some kind of joke?!'

He felt as if the world were ending.

'Did you just turn me into a woman? I'm here to remove my appendix.'

Blurry images of white consternation darted about. Commotion, chaos, convening, conferring. Someone ran over and said that the person who wanted a sex-change operation had been wheeled into the room next door.

'Is this some kind of joke?!' he wailed again. At the same time, he felt a pain in the area they'd operated on. The anaesthesia faded real fast.

He insisted that he wanted to go back to being a man.

'Won't recommend that. Too dangerous.'

He didn't care, he didn't care, and he didn't care. In any case, it was their mistake. They needed to take responsibility for their actions and return him to what he was.

The anaesthesiologist gave him an injection.

2.

Everything was dazzlingly white when he woke up. Strong white light, white clouds, white fog, men and women in white gowns.

White is the colour of holiness.

He smiled and asked, 'Am I back to what I was?'

They replied, smiling, 'You're back. The operation was not successful. '

'Is this some kind of joke?! What is this place? Why did you bring me here? I was operated on at the hospital!'

An expanse of white understanding, serenity, and peacefulness materialised before him. Someone in a white gown came over and spoke to the others. They were also in white gowns.

'Oh, I recognise him,' he said. 'He was the one we made a blunder on the last time.'

'Is this some kind of joke?!' he wailed. At the same time, he was appalled that he could no longer feel pain in the area they'd operated on.

The person in white said, 'You were supposed to be a woman the previous time. We made a mistake and made you a man. By a stroke of luck, we now have a chance to make amends this time round. To do it all over again.'

He insisted that he was basically a man. If he could no longer be a man, then he would rather not be human.

They didn't care, they didn't care, and they gently didn't care. But in any case, it was 'originally' their fault, so they would take full responsibility.

The person in the white gown, the one with a pair of wings, gave him an injection.

FOREVER (MY) BUTTERFLY

The sky broke open just then. The rain poured down on the asphalt road, covering it with a cold, glistening sheen. They ducked under the sheltered corridor of the shophouses. He was wearing a white windbreaker, looking at the green postbox on this side of the street. Even though they stood side by side, I felt that he was alone. Yingzi looked over here too. She knew that I'd been standing behind the shop window the whole time.

Why aren't they talking? They've been silent for a while.

Even though a road separated us, I could see Yingzi from here. She had a determined expression on her face, though her lips were trembling. At that moment, he spoke to her. She froze before opening her mouth to reply. He nodded his head in silence, reaching into his windbreaker pocket and giving her an envelope.

Yingzi smiled at him and spoke again. She opened her umbrella and crossed the road to the postbox on my side of the street. As far as I was concerned, she was walking towards me.

I saw the look in Yingzi's eyes—she noticed me. Now she headed towards me, her back to him. For the past six months, she'd been opening her heart to me and shutting him out. Yingzi gave me a smile. The look on her face seemed to say: *let me do one last thing for him. Then I'll let him know.*

Then a high-pitched screech from a braking car. Yingzi's life flitted into the air and, softly, fell back onto the cold and wet asphalt, as if she were a butterfly swallowed up by the night.

Even though it was spring, it felt like a late autumn day.

She was crossing the road to post a letter for him. That's all. A simple act that will stay in my memory forever. I opened my eyes as slowly as possible. From behind the shop window, burning tears welled up in my eyes as I was overcome by devastation. All the cars in the world came to a halt, and a crowd gathered in the middle of the road. To him, it was five metres of forever. For me, it was forever a distance of merely five metres. He must have deeply regretted letting her go five metres from him. As for me, I could only grieve in my heart over the five metres I'd forever have to go before I could be like him, carrying Yingzi in his arms in broad daylight for everyone to see.

The raindrops pelted against the shop window, radiating outward upon impact, like ripples in water. Although the clear glass separated us, it was as if the deluge was pouring into my life.

Then I saw her again—an eternal Yingzi—wearing a white windbreaker, opening her umbrella, quietly crossing the road. The Yingzi whom he loved has become his butterfly forever. The Yingzi whom I loved has also become mine forever, in my own way. The whole world could be swarming towards the Yingzi lying on the road, but they'd never be able to enter the secret garden that belonged to only the butterfly and me—this secret garden that everyone might have come to know. I stood behind the shop window, my mind in a fog, guarding this secret for Yingzi. I had helped him realise his forever with Yingzi, but at the same time, sealed away my own forever with her.

Young Yingzi hadn't known what was in that letter, but I did. I was his best friend. Two days ago, he'd told me that he and Yingzi had decided to get married next month, and the letter was to inform his mother of the good news. I'd wanted to come clean with him because of this, but the kind-hearted Yingzi had pleaded with me to let her tell him herself so as not to cause him even more pain.

We had arranged to do it today at this place where they usually rendezvoused. She would let him know. It just happened to be raining today. I'd even been thinking about rainy days and farewells—how they are forever meant for each other.

DESCENDANTS

That day, he took some time during the lesson to read his student Huang Zhongren's essay to the class.

The essay was titled *My Family*. The student had a pretty good grasp of Chinese, but he chose to read the essay not because he wanted the class to learn from Zhongren, but rather to avoid doing what Zhongren had done.

This was how the essay went: *I have a very special family. My paternal grandpa, my father, and me—all from three different generations—have different surnames.*

The whole class listened attentively.

My paternal grandpa's surname is Tan, but in actual fact, his surname was Wong. According to my father, when Grandpa first arrived in Singapore many years ago, he went and joined the queue at the National Registration Department to register his name. The person in charge of putting down his surname in English had asked my grandpa what his surname was. As my grandpa only spoke Cantonese, he didn't understand what the person was saying in English at all. So, in barely passable Hokkien, he answered, 'Wait.' The word wait in Hokkien sounded like Tan, which the other person misinterpreted as the surname Tan. From then on, my grandpa's surname became Tan.

The whole class roared with laughter. The teacher continued.

When it was my father's turn to pick up his identity card, my family finally got back our actual surname, Wong. Father said something like, 'Lucky my surname's Wong again. Otherwise, people will keep calling me Mr. Tan everywhere I go.'

The whole class laughed so hard that tears rolled down their cheeks. The teacher read the last few sentences of the essay.

After I was born, my family became the Huang family. That's because people from my generation use the standard Mandarin Chinese phonetic system known as Hanyu Pinyin to spell our surnames, which changed my surname from Wong to Huang. That's my family in a nutshell.

The teacher tried to make himself heard amidst the peals of laughter, saying they should focus on the essay's subject.

In a grave tone, he continued. 'We're all Chinese people. The Chinese have an idiom that asks us, as "huang zhong ren", people of Chinese descent, not to forget our ancestors. It's especially interesting if we apply the idiom "dan huang zi sun" here in this student's case. Doesn't that sound very much like "tan huang zi sun"?'

A student raised his hand.

'Sir, "dan huang"? Like the egg yolk ah? I mean, yolk is pronounced as "dan huang", no?' he asked.

The teacher frowned and wrote the four Chinese characters dan huang zi sun on the board, which literally meant 'descendants in pale yellow' in English. He made the students copy it down in their books:

淡黄子孙.

Note: The Chinese idiom referred to in the story as 'dan huang zi sun' 淡黄子孙 should be 'yan huang zi sun' 炎黄子孙, which means 'descendants of the Chinese people'. However, in the story, the teacher has also written it wrongly. He has written the first character 炎 'yan' as 淡 'dan'.

THE THINKER

It's just wild that such a refined gentleman can be so brazen when it comes to farting.

The man lives next door. Well, then again, he might not actually *live* there, as I've never seen him stay the night in the flat. Since a year ago, he's been coming to the flat every afternoon and lingering for two hours or so before leaving. When we run into each other in the lift or the corridor, he'll nod his head and smile. But we've never said a single word to each other.

At first, I thought he might be keeping a mistress in the flat. But I've never seen any other person enter or leave. He may very well be a wolf in sheep's clothing for all I know: he looks all civil and genteel, but perhaps beneath the façade lurks a vicious drug smuggler who rents the unit to hide his illegal loot.

One day, I even climbed out my back window onto the ledge and peeped into his flat. To my surprise, there was nothing inside. It was completely bare, except for a few balls of crumpled paper strewn around in the corner of the room.

Our building isn't well insulated. The array of sounds in the building ranges from neighbours talking, quarrelling, sneezing, and snoring to neighbours hitting their kids, playing mahjong, and flushing the toilet. All this pandemonium can be heard through the walls loud and clear. Occasionally, I even hear the frisky middle-aged couple upstairs moaning in pleasure, even though they tend to look very intense and solemn when they leave their flat.

Obviously, no such sounds come from that man's flat. The only sounds I hear from that flat are all manner of farts.

Farting sounds have become very rare in our city. Ever since it was awarded the 'No Rubbish City' title a decade ago, it has become deeply obsessed with cleanliness. It didn't help that it went on to win a No Smoking City award five years later. Then just last year, someone proposed an initiative to discourage people from farting. Naturally, it caused fierce debate in parliament.

Even though Parliament hasn't passed a law forbidding people from farting in public places, many people have responded, or adapted, to the proposal with much fervour. Some companies and schools led the way and held No Farting campaigns. After all, it isn't very civic-minded to fart in public places. Loud farts block our hearing and stinky farts impede our smelling. In general, farts tarnish the image of the city, so it's best that they are prohibited once and for all.

But with all the fart ban furore, it's become exceptionally rare to hear even one resounding fart from the man next door. 'PPP... OOOOO...T'. This sound, every gradation of which rings loud and clear at a regular time every day, used to make me frown. But after a while, I've actually found myself longing for it whenever the man isn't in his flat.

Once, when the sound of PPP...OOOOO...T hit me again from next door, I couldn't help but climb out my back window to sneak a peek. I saw him, hands behind his back, an air of elegance about him, pacing up and down the flat. Now and then he would let out a fart and halt, write something on a sheet of paper on the floor, then continue to pace up and down, farting here and there.

I've only found out recently that the man, a world-class thinker, is held in high regard by this city—considered a national treasure, to be exact. I didn't know him through his books but I got to know him from watching TV last week. The news reported that this thinker and his family were honoured with the city's first ever No Farting Family award for their successful voluntary efforts to quit farting. The credit went to the thinker's wife who, in front of the camera, shared how their whole family had eradicated farting from their minds within a year simply through her strict rules and unrelenting no-no's.

The thinker didn't say a word. He was his usual reticent, refined self. He only smiled at the camera.

I was a bit surprised to notice a secret basking in his radiant smile of glory. Thing is, I have been blessed with the brilliance of the thinker's secret too. From then on, for two hours in the afternoon every day, I have begun to be extremely mindful of his sacred and dignified 'PPP…OOOOO…T'.

SHORT STORY

We've been married for three years, but this is the first time I'm accompanying Zhiqiang to see a friend. I blame it on the coffee at breakfast this morning.

Zhiqiang was drinking his coffee when he said, 'Know something about the ex-classmate I'm meeting this evening? You won't believe his name. He's called Xiaoshuo in Chinese, which translates into something like *story* or *novel* in English. Happens that this guy's pretty challenged in height too. That year, we had this new English teacher who said something like 'Oh! What a short Story!' when he stood up during roll call. And that was it. From then on, everyone called him Short Story.'

'Classy,' I said. 'Even his entrance has the elements of a story. I'd like to meet this ex-classmate of yours.'

'You should go back to your poems and essays. I mean, novels are much too stirring for you.'

This last remark made me bristle. So now both of us are here in the café where Zhiqiang is supposed to meet Story.

He is indeed short. Definitely not a looker: small eyes, flat nose. He doesn't even look at me when he says to Zhiqiang: 'I wanted to meet you alone.'

I'm not offended, though. On our way there, Zhiqiang has already told me that his ex-classmate's a weirdo. We're just about to explain ourselves when Story starts to speak in a tone reminiscent of Milan Kundera's interspersed flashbacks.

'Forget it. Forget it. The character has more right to speak than the author.'

We can't be bothered to make sense of what he's just said. Instead, we sit down and order some tea.

Without beating around the bush, Zhiqiang asks Story, 'We haven't met for so long. So why are you thinking of me now?'

'There are two versions of this story. Version one: I've recently switched to selling insurance. I was going through my list of exclassmates and saw your name. As for why I've switched jobs…'

I cut him short. 'I'd like to hear version two.'

Story looks at me for the first time. His piercing gaze seems to see through me, and he starts to speak to me in a gruff voice.

'So you've chosen this for yourself. A choice fastened to another choice, branching out again and again. A story's a tree of choices, and so is life. A fleeting thought makes an enduring decision. Every choice is irreversible.'

The waiter serves our tea. Zhiqiang can't take his eyes off his cup, whereas I refuse to back down on version two. I fix my gaze on Story. 'Version two.'

'Alright.' He switches to the tone men like to use for talking about men's business. Looking at Zhiqiang, he says: 'Do you remember that night in Hong Kong when we had a meeting? Two months ago?'

Zhiqiang sips his tea. His eyes narrow.

'Let me think.'

His memory has always been terrible.

Story acts as if he's a doctor trying to guide an amnesiac into remembering things. He emphasises every word. 'That. Bar. Called. Dream.'

Stunned, I turn to Zhiqiang.

'You go to bars?'

'No. Not really. But, that night, I think some friend suggested going…' He sounds very uncertain.

'You went,' Story says. 'Your friend made you. When you got there, he hooked up with a Caucasian girl and left without you. After that, someone came and chatted you up. Both of you hit it off pretty well.'

Zhiqiang looks like he's remembered something. 'Now that you say so, it seems to be coming back to me.'

Story continues. 'You didn't go back to the hotel that night. You went back to his place and spent a romantic night with him.'

It's beyond belief.

'What utter bullshit!' I blurt out.

I've never yelled at someone using those words before.

Zhiqiang tries his very best to recall what happened. 'Are you sure? I think I went back to my hotel…'

Story continues to wire-pull Zhiqiang's memory.

'You don't remember? He had a mirrored ceiling in his bedroom. You even saw the red mole on his butt.'

Zhiqiang sighs. 'Oh, them. I remember now…'

The many twists in the plot are so preposterous that I don't even know where to begin. My voice drips with hatred as I say coldly to Zhiqiang, 'Well done.'

Zhiqiang looks at Story blankly, giving ear to him, all dazed and stupefied.

'Do you want to know who that person is?' asks Story. 'Version one: it's my younger female cousin. Last week, she mentioned how much she missed Zhiqiang—that's how I found out about this. She's flying in tomorrow.'

I have no intention of hearing him continue his story, but my way of stopping him from going further is a tad foolish.

'Version two!' I blurt.

'The story's the same. Well, except it wasn't my younger female cousin but my younger male cousin.'

I can't control the volume of my voice anymore. I stare at Zhiqiang, livid with anger.

'Say something. What do you have to say?'

Zhiqiang stammers and mutters a few words. Story speaks in his stead.

'Version one. He asks you to forgive him. It was a moment of folly on his part. In fact, he doesn't know why he acted that way that night…'

'Version two!' I spit out those two words like I'm under a curse.

Zhiqiang is suddenly charged with steely resolve. He doesn't look at me. I have this feeling that he can't see me anymore. In my ears, I can only hear what he is saying to Story.

'Xiaoshuo, take me back to the "xiaoshuo". Give me the story you want me to have. It's my fault. I shouldn't have escaped to real life. Reality's bland as plain water. I remember what role I should be playing now. Take me back into the "xiaoshuo", please.'

I sweep the teacups off the table. They fall to the floor, shattering to pieces. Just like my heart. But I'm not broken. I stand up and address Zhiqiang.

'You piece of shit. Do you know what you're saying?'

A forced smile crawls across Story's face.

'He knows what he's saying. I've already given him some character flaws. You too. You chose to come here today, even though I've been meaning to do away with a minor character like you. Sorry I didn't flesh you out properly.'

The whole thing is so ridiculous—bordering on outrageous, really—that I turn and walk away. Tossing Zhiqiang away is like tossing a dress away. I can still hear Story behind me.

'You will keep walking. You will never come back. You will disappear from Zhiqiang's life. I'm sorry I never even did a character sketch for you.'

All of a sudden, I want to turn back. I want to look into Zhiqiang's eyes, to see those eyes filled with remorse, but my legs won't hear of it. My personality as a character is dictating my actions. Before leaving the cafe, I begin to wonder whether Story really does have a say in my character development. Then I become very concerned about how careful he has been in designing my image and personality in the story. However, as soon as I step out the door, my awareness goes poof. I'm blank.

The end.

A POTATO DATE

I waited in the room for a long time before he finally walked in. There was a glow about him.

After he latched the door, I asked, 'Feeling good today?'

He gave me a smile, as usual.

'Not too bad.'

He took a seat. On the table lay the medical history form, but we both pretended it didn't exist. One, I'm already very familiar with his condition. Two, I don't want him to feel that this is our regular consultation session.

'Regarding what we talked about last time, I hope you didn't tell anyone?'

'No, I didn't. With things like this, it's better that less people know.'

We kept our voices very low, lest the people outside hear us. We had an unspoken understanding between us¬—such was our chemistry.

'I'll tell you a secret. I discovered quite a few potatoes here.'

'Quite a few?'

'Yeah. Though, I wasn't as shocked as when I found out that I was a potato myself.'

'Wow, you're sharp as a tack these days.'

We almost laughed out loud but managed to control ourselves.

'So you were telling me last time that you discovered you were a potato while looking into the restroom mirror? Did I get that right?'

'Right. I had been working in the office for two consecutive days and nights. When I submitted my report, the boss threw it back at me and gave me a dressing down. For a moment I felt like I was covered in ashes, you know. It was that dispiriting. I went to the office restroom to wash my face, and when I lifted my head from the sink, I couldn't see my face anymore. There was just a potato looking back at me.'

'Yes, you told me that before.'

'Well, last time I forgot to say that half the skin on my face was peeled off. The other half looked like it'd fall off any minute.'

'Like a naked potato?'

'Yeah, stark naked. I went back to my seat and tried my best to act like nothing had happened. But I felt so cold. It was like I didn't have clothes on. My colleagues were exchanging dirty jokes in a corner, cackling like there were no other people around them. I know for a fact that they were speaking in code. They were laughing at me, no doubt.'

'Perhaps not?'

'I was one hundred percent sure. Soon after, I realised that some of them were also potatoes. They just didn't know it yet. Laughing potatoes are so pathetic.'

'Is that why the last time we saw each other, you said you weren't going to eat french fries ever again?'

'But of course. To be cut into long, thin strips? Oh my. You can't even see the potato's original form. And then the potatoes are deep fried into their final form, looking exactly the same to everyone who's stuffing them down their throats. If anyone wants french fries, the fries have to satisfy their demands immediately. Even though I'm a potato, I still gotta be a potato with backbone.'

'Shhhh, don't let anyone hear that.'

'Ok, back to what's happening here. I'll tell you a secret. You know the lady wearing glasses at the reception desk outside? She's a potato. To be more exact, she's a silent potato.'

'Wow, even potatoes have personalities.'

'Exactly. They can't escape my detection. There are still quite a few potatoes that report here every day. Like the one standing guard at the main door; the one controlling the buttons in the lift. Oh, and even one or two wearing white robes.'

'My, my. Your eyes are becoming very sharp. You can even see that.'

'Well, at first I needed to see their reflections in the mirror, but not anymore. I can see at first glance if they're a potato in human skin. I just keep my mouth shut; I don't want to expose them. Of course, there's a chance that they don't know they're potatoes either.'

'Time's up.'

'Exactly. When the time's up, I'll expose them.'

'No, I mean, time's up for us.'

'Oh, we'll talk again next time, then. Remember, don't tell anyone what I told you. Just in case people panic.'

Before he left through the door, I reminded him.

'Remember, take your pills twice a day.'

As he opened the door, he turned back and smiled. His usual smile.

Before he closed the door, I heard him whisper to someone outside.

'Keep an eye on him.'

KEPT

She let me in. As soon as the door was closed, she tore at my belt like a cat in heat.

This got me very excited, and I, with practised skill, started to unbutton her blouse.

'You know what I want.'

She had already unbuckled my belt before I'd managed to unbutton her blouse all the way. Very gently, she unzipped my trousers.

'Quick, give it to me.'

I carried her in my arms, lay her on the bed, and climbed on top of her.

'Say it. Say you love me.'

Silence.

'You know what I want.'

She mounted me again. She had to do this every time, otherwise she wouldn't be satisfied.

'Quick, give it to me.'

The ceiling was covered with mirrors, as if specially designed for me to savour her poses and study my movements.

'Say it. Say you love me.'

In the mirrors, I could see our aroused bodies moving in synchronicity, submerged in ecstasy, reaching the height of our pleasure.

Silence.

'You know what I want.'

She lay on the bed, quiet, not wanting to move.

I stood up, buck naked, and walked to the parrot's perch as usual.

'Quick, give it to me.'

With practised skill, I scooped up some parrot feed and put it into the small feeding dish on the stand. The parrot pecked at it hastily. If it started to peck at someone with its sharp beak, I bet it would be very painful for that person.

'Say it. Say you love me.'

Silence.

As I was about to leave, she closed her eyes before opening the door for me.

'You know what I want.'

With practised skill, I kissed her forehead.

'Quick, give it to me.'

I held her tightly. We both knew that we wouldn't be able to cling to each other like this forever.

Before she closed the door, I could still hear the parrot talking.

'Say it. Say you love me.'

The mafia boss keeps the parrot as a pet. She's his kept woman. I'm her kept man.

I've heard that the mafia boss keeps a parrot to keep her entertained, but the parrot, having learned to mimic what people say, does more than just dispel boredom.

We've never exchanged a single word in that house. She needs to be the master puppeteer controlling each and every movement, but she also needs the excitement that comes with spontaneous risk-taking.

Looks like the mafia boss who's keeping her wants to have words to go hand in hand with the action. She's probably quiet most of the time so, each visit, what I'm hearing is the parrot reading its scripted lines—mimicking what that man says—again and again.

'You know what I want.'

'Quick, give it to me.'

'Say it. Say you love me.'

THREE JOURNAL ENTRIES FOR HOMEWORK

1.

The weather was great today. I went out with my mother early in the morning. In the lift, we bumped into the uncle living next door with his kid. There was a woman with them holding the kid's hand. The kid called her 'Auntie'. My mother once told me that this auntie is from the Philippines and even has a university degree. 'What's university?' I remember asking my mother. My mother said I'd know what a university was when I started going to one. She then told the uncle that his wife was a very smart woman. In fact, she found out from watching the news yesterday that his wife was out of town again for a meeting. The uncle smiled but didn't answer. He merely turned to the kid's auntie and reminded her to take the kid to music class in the afternoon.

Teacher's feedback: Vague expressions. I can't make head or tail of this. Please remember to use paragraphs.

2.

The weather was good today. On our way home, my mother and I bumped into the uncle living next door when the lift door opened. Uncle's kid is already quite big, tall even, but he still wanted his auntie to carry him! The auntie carried the kid in her arms so he could reach Uncle to give him a kiss. My mother commented to Uncle that he and his kid were very close. Uncle was very happy. He said that the kid was even closer to his auntie. Before Uncle went into the lift, he told the kid's auntie that he had to work overtime that night so they should go to bed first. The auntie took the kid home, and I went home with my mother. I asked my mother why she told me not to call that lady 'Auntie'. My mother said I shouldn't be calling the man Uncle while calling the lady 'Auntie' in front of him. It was very rude. But the kid also called her 'Auntie', I told her.

My mother replied that if she said not to call the lady 'Auntie', then could I please not call her 'Auntie'.

Teacher's feedback: Unclear use of language. I think I've read this journal entry before. Come see me, please.

3.

The weather was wonderful today. I went out with my mother early in the morning. In the lift, we bumped into the uncle living next door with his kid. The kid's auntie was also with them. The kid let his auntie hold his hand while the Uncle stooped down so the kid could give him a kiss. After that, the kid, with his hand in his auntie's, went with the auntie to the market. The kid's auntie asked the uncle to come back home earlier that night. The uncle smiled at her very happily and walked off. After we got on the bus, my mother told me that I would be allowed to call that lady 'Auntie' the next time I saw her. I asked her how come? Why is it that I can call her 'Auntie' now like the kid does? My mother said that me calling her 'Auntie' and the kid calling her 'Auntie' meant two very different things, and that wasn't the end of it. There's now a difference between the kid calling her 'Auntie' in the past and the kid calling her 'Auntie' in the present. I was so confused. My mother said that I'll understand when I'm in university.

Teacher's feedback: Unclear use of language. I think I've graded this entry before. You are so slack. Redo this.

EYES

I've just moved into my new home and I'm very happy with it, especially the balcony. I have my breakfast on the balcony every morning, admiring the scenery as I eat.

As time goes by, I realise the scenery that's most affecting to me isn't in front of me or far away in the distance—it's to my right, on the balcony of the unit next door but one floor higher. Every morning, I see three old people sunbathing on the balcony with sunglasses perched on their noses. Sometimes they laugh at each other's words, sometimes they read their newspapers without a sound. There is one old man and two old women. When they're together, the old man often sits between the two women, one woman on each side. One time, I saw the woman on the left peeling melon seeds for the old man, but he gave the peeled melon seeds to the woman on the right. There was this other time when he gave an apple to the woman on the right, but the woman gave it to the woman on the left. Every so often, both old women giggle at the old man's jokes. And they're usually so tickled that they bury their heads in his chest at the same time.

In any case, it's the very picture of a loving couple, even though it's three people, not two.

One day, unable to suppress my curiosity any longer, I try to coax some information from a neighbour: what kind of relationship do those three people have? The lady next door says that the two women are the old man's lovers. That gets me even more intrigued, so I press on: there are lovers this old? Also, the three lovers are living together under the same roof in apparent harmony, and they even seem to be more loving than ever?

'Oh, don't you know?' she says. 'The three of them share one pair of eyes.'

One pair of eyes? I'm sceptical. She continues, saying that many years ago, in their youth, the three of them were in a tragic love triangle. The man couldn't bear to let either woman go, and the two women couldn't stand the sight of each other. Neither was willing to back off. Finally, the man drove the two women somewhere to talk, but they got into a car accident. They found out about the cornea damage when they regained consciousness.

'The man's cornea, right?' I ask. 'And both women probably feel guilty?'

'No. It was the two women.'

'So…then what?'

'Well, then the man privately arranged for his pair of corneas to be donated to his two lady companions: one cornea for each soulmate. One eye looks at the other eye, and both eyes belong to the lover. How could they possibly see any enmity? Don't you agree?'

'The two people would, of course, shower that one person with even more love. Three people, three times the affection!'

From this point on, I become even more moved by the scenery from my balcony. They continue to wear their sunglasses every day. Day after day, they wear the same style of sunglasses and keep the same sort of routine. Three people sharing one pair of eyes.

Whenever the two old women look affectionately at the napping old man from behind their sunglasses, speechless, I think: look at that pair of eyes gazing speechlessly at their own happiness.

A CRICKET

'A cricket!'

He almost shouted, but of course, he didn't.

He wore a tie and a pair of shiny leather shoes. His fingers were clasped around a briefcase handle. He couldn't have anything to do with crickets, even though, in his mind, they shared a bond.

Nonetheless, he heard a cricket chirping. *Chirp. Chirrp. Chirrrrrrp.* The sound was definitely coming from within the lift. *Impossible.* His face betrayed nothing, but he sneaked a peek at his neighbours, packed in with him like sardines. Some were off to work; some were off to school. They looked exactly the same as they did yesterday, and every single day, in fact. Their eyes were fixed on the glowing numbers descending in leaps on the lift indicator panel; their expressions were cold and stony.

No one realised that there was a cricket in the lift, except him. He could very well be wrong. Perhaps it was his mind playing tricks on him, convincing him that he was hearing a chirping cricket. The lift reached the ground floor. Everyone streamed out of the lift. These were neighbours that he saw every day, and yet, it felt as if he never saw them. He purposely waited for everyone to leave the lift until he was the only one left. Before he walked out, he looked around the lift again. *No damn crickets. I must have heard wrongly.*

When he finally left the lift, he saw a foreign domestic helper give him a curious stare. He then realised that it really was very strange for him to stay behind in the lift, looking for invisible crickets.

When he returned home from work late at night, he took the lift alone, feeling exhausted. He was the only person in the lift. As usual, he started to loosen his tie. Then he heard the cricket again. He felt a shot of rejuvenation electrify his whole body, dispelling the fatigue clogging his pores. Listening carefully, he confirmed that it was indeed a cricket. Perhaps, in the still of the night, the cricket's chirping was all the more distinct. *Chirp. Chirrp. Chirrrrrrp.* He listened to the chirping, following it to its source. It sounded like it was coming from the air vent.

Is a cricket trapped in the utter darkness of the lift motor room? Chirp. Chirrp. Chirrrrrrp. Is it crying softly for help? He started to panic on the invisible cricket's behalf. However, when the lift door opened, the chirping vanished. Again.

After he got home, he took a shower, changed his clothes, and went to bed like he always did. As usual, he gave his wife a kiss, switched off the light, and closed his eyes. His weariness was so familiar that it lulled him to sleep almost immediately. Before too long, he heard chirping again. *A cricket!* He sat up at once, prompting his wife to switch on the light.

'What's wrong?'

'Did you hear that?'

'What am I supposed to hear?'

He listened carefully, but he couldn't hear the chirping anymore. Had it been a dream?

He lay down again and switched off the light. In the dark, he told his wife that he'd heard a cricket chirping in the lift today, and that it had been loud and had gone like this: *Chirp. Chirrp. Chirrrrrrp.* He was certain that it had been a cricket.

'A cricket? I've never seen a cricket in my life.'

That's true, he thought to himself. He'd never seen a cricket in his life either. So how would he know for sure that it was a cricket that he'd heard? He tried hard to listen for it again but only heard the steady breathing of his wife in deep slumber.

From that day onwards, he was a man with a secret—a secret between a cricket and him. It felt as if he was betraying the whole apartment building with this tiny secret. Or, perhaps, one could even say that he had betrayed the whole city. Every morning, his neighbours, veiled behind their vacant expressions, continued to go to work or school. They didn't see the smile lifting the corners of his mouth. That was the common understanding he had with the cricket. Every day, he rushed back home. Or rather, before going back home, he rushed to the lift to enjoy his time with the cricket. Actually, that's not right either. Rather, he rushed to the lift to bask in the exultation of a rendezvous with the chirping cricket.

Chirp. Chirrp. Chirrrrrrp. It was a cricket for sure. He was certain that within the chirping, he could hear blades of grass rustling. Or should he say, fields of grass. Green grass. Blue sky. Had he ever had, or had he ever belonged to, green grass and blue sky? He thought he had once, but not in this city. And not him but his Ah Pa. His Pa had told him about the days he spent catching crickets in his hometown when he was small.

Where was the hometown? He couldn't see it. There was only a solitary him and a solitary cricket in the lift, day after day, hiding away from the world. As time passed, the lift became a sort of hometown to him because there was a cricket in it. Well, at least to him, there was a cricket.

Day after day.

He didn't know how many days had passed, because every day was the same. Every person he met was the same, except him, except the cricket. *Chirp. Chirrp. Chirrrrrrp.* There's a cricket hiding inside me. In the office. *Chirp. Chirrp. Chirrrrrrp.* In the conference hall. *Chirp. Chirrp. Chirrrrrrp.* In the MRT train. *Chirp. Chirrp. Chirrrrrrp.*

One night, in his sleep, he dreamt that the chirping in the lift had vanished. He sat up straight and his wife, bleary-eyed, asked what was wrong. He didn't answer. He switched on the light, got out of bed, left the bedroom, opened the door, and ran to the lift. He pressed the lift button. After a while, the door opened and he walked in. No sound. He tried to prick up his ears again. There was really no sound. He tried harder. He finally confirmed that there was no sound at all.

The cricket is no longer here.

He went back to his flat, crestfallen. In the bedroom, his wife asked, 'What's wrong now?'

'I really hope this is a dream. And when I wake from this dream, I hope the cricket's still there.'

He carried on talking and talking. After some time, he woke up.

When he opened his eyes, he was elated to find himself in the lift motor room, cloaked in absolute darkness. A cricket was trapped in some impassive building of some impassive city. *I don't know why I can't get out.*

Chirp. Chirrp. Chirrrrrrp.

DREAM INTERPRETATION

'When the bride extended her hand to shake mine, I got a fright.'

We had our main meal first. Afterwards, a plate of rambutans was served as dessert.

'I'm not eating those. I hate rambutans. They don't have much flesh, but if you throw them away uneaten, it's a waste of money. And it's no guarantee that they're sweet! But if you eat them, your hands get sticky.'

She kept on talking, but gradually changed the subject to a dream that she'd recently had.

In the dream, she'd been standing in front of a pair of newlyweds. The groom was someone she knew, but not very well.

'What's he like?' I asked.

'Well, like…um, well, forgettable. An average man on the street you're likely to forget if you don't see him for a long time.'

In her dream, the man had taken the initiative and extended his hand with a smile. She, on the other hand, had felt obliged to shake the groom's hand as way of congratulating him. She'd also wanted to give her blessings to his bride, who was standing next to him. The bride had been an average-looking, forgettable woman you'd likely forget if you hadn't seen her for a long time.

'When the bride extended her hand to shake mine, I got a fright.'

I took a rambutan from the plate. Before I could finish peeling it, my curiosity got the better of me, so I asked, 'What was wrong?'

'Her hand. Oh gosh. How should I describe it? I mean, you could still see her palm and fingers, but her skin was hairy and coarse. It was like some sort of fruit, like…' Her eyes fell on the rambutan in my hand. 'Like rambutan skin.'

'What a strange dream,' I said.

She then told me that, in the dream, she'd been looking at the smiling man as if she were in a daze. Then she'd said to him, 'You are so…' and woke up.

Now she looked at me. 'Can you please interpret the dream?'

'So, the man's very ordinary?'

She nodded.

'And the woman was just as ordinary?'

She nodded.

'You can't stand rambutans, you say?'

She nodded without hesitation.

Without warning, I gently tossed the rambutan into the air. It fell towards her. She let out a 'Yikes!' and instinctively reached for it. Before the mass of black shadow managed to end up on the floor, she had already caught it.

'There. That's the meaning of your dream.'

I picked up another rambutan and started to peel it slowly.

TWO QUESTIONS FROM THE CLASSICS

The Assassination of Emperor Qin

Emperor Qin ducked between the massive pillars, sweating profusely as he ran for his life. Warriors dashed to the palace to escort him to safety. Jingke knew there was no time to lose—he had one last chance to strike. The dagger in his hand was short, but the risk incurred in killing Emperor Qin was high. The span of history is vast, but the time of a hero is brief.

He would throw the dagger. It would be a wistful throw—a final blow that would go down in history, and which generations would replay in their minds over and over. Jingke suddenly sensed Emperor Qin slowing down. The warriors also slowed their steps. There were only a few seconds left, but no one kept up their pace. Except him.

That was his only chance—his very last chance—at a fresh start. Jingke aimed at Emperor Qin. Just as he was about to throw the dagger, he caught a look. *The susurration of the wind, the frostiness of the Yishui River.* A parting look as beautiful as a poem. A look that has repeated itself across generations whenever people have bid one another farewell.

Finally, Jingke realised what his dagger needed to strike, or rather, what it need not strike. Emperor Qin would soon regain his speed. The warriors would soon regain their speed. At that very moment, he threw the dagger with every ounce of skill he had mastered, with all the strength left in him.

Leaves fell, striking the Yishui River for all eternity.

Huarong Pass

At the Huarong Pass, Guan Yu studied the wretchedness of Cao Cao's expression again and again. Cao Cao too studied the hesitation in Guan Yu's expression again and again.

As he approached, the white-faced Cao Cao saw the valiant Guan Yu blocking his way such that he could no longer advance.

He bowed ever so slightly. 'Lord Guan, I plead with you to recall the kindness I've shown you in the past and to let me go.'

The red-faced Guan Yu said: 'Let you go? How will I be able to face my elder brother thereafter? How will I be able to face the people?'

Onstage, White Face pleaded hundreds and thousands of times with Red Face. Red Face's heart softened hundreds and thousands of times for White Face. The audience held their breath. This was the troupe's most exciting show, and all credit went to White Face and Red Face's consummate performance—their chemistry was amazing.

When Cao Cao saw Guan Yu bend slightly to one side and let out a long sigh, he hastily waved to his soldiers and crept past the hesitant Guan Yu. When Guan Yu closed his eyes, Cao Cao suddenly saw the piteous expression on Guan Yu's face when he'd once asked him for money. *I'm going to die, dear Mengde. Save me, please.* He'd almost forgotten how many times Lord Guan had said that to him.

'Where do you think you're going!'

The red-faced Guan Yu opened his eyes and yelled at Cao Cao as he attempted to flee. The audience roared with approval at their superb performance. Amid the applause, white-faced Cao Cao looked paler than a sheet of white paper. His body trembling and his voice quivering, he said, 'Lord Guan, I plead with you to recall the grace I once showed you. Without it, you'd never have gone on to surmount every hurdle in life…'

Red Face plunged the Green Dragon Crescent Blade upright into the ground, his will wavering again. A hero's weakness was especially enchanting. 'Kill! Kill! Kill!' the audience shouted. White Face stared at Red Face. He recalled how he'd wanted to kill him when he'd seen his blushing wife through the crack in the door. On top of his wife, Red Face had kept his eyes closed.

It was Cao Cao's turn to plead for mercy. He had rehearsed this excellent scene again and again in his head. White Face needed to say his last words. Why had he been born with the face of a villain? He really didn't want to plead with Red Face again even though, without Red Face, he would lose the reputation he'd built up at the playhouse over the years. The troupe director had also told him in private that Red Face's image must not be tarnished. 'No matter what, the livelihoods of our many brothers in the troupe can't be affected. Not to mention their families,' the director had said.

'Kill! Kill! Kill!' Amid the audience's shouts, Cao Cao had to open his mouth and say the lines he'd rehearsed many times in his head. 'Lord Guan. Please. Please spare me!' The troupe director had said to him in a low voice: *spare him.*

But white-faced Cao Cao saw himself in the eyes of red-faced Guan Yu. There was a raging fire in his eyes. The fire, a scarlet red. His wife's face, blushing and burning. The flames were red. The face was red.

For the last time, Red Face had said: 'Lend me the money, please. If you don't help me, I'll die.'

'I'm dying,' his wife had moaned to Red Face, her breath heavy like she was heaving for air.

'Lord Guan. Please. Please…just kill me!' pleaded Cao Cao.

At the Huarong Pass, Guan Yu's Green Dragon Crescent Blade wavered in confusion at the unfamiliar lines. Beside the Huarong Pass, countless faces in the audience were dumbstruck.

LOOKING FOR A LION

It was already the seventh day. They arrived at the only rest stop in the National Wildlife Park. As they were getting out of the safari vehicle, he stood up and held out his warm hand for her. Gently, he put her hand into his so she could step down from the vehicle with ease.

This was the only place they were allowed to stop and walk around. Just as they had done every day for the past six days, they took a seat in the open-air courtyard where tea was sold.

'Let me get the tea today,' he said.

He walked to the tea kiosk with a slow and collected gait, his back tall and straight like an alpha male. She smiled, thinking that he must want to return the favour since she'd been the one buying him tea for the last six days.

She'd come from so far away and her only wish on this safari was to see a South African male lion. On the first day, before he'd started driving, he'd told her not to get out of the vehicle or make any noise, else she startle the animals and endanger herself.

She'd listened to him quietly and told him that she wanted only to see the lion. He'd laughed.

'There are lions, but it depends on your luck. There was one old lady who only wanted to see elephants. They're actually very common and not a rare sight at all. But somehow she didn't see a single elephant for the whole five days, even though she saw rhinos, zebras, hippos, giraffes and buffalos every day, day and night; just no elephants! As for lions, it really depends on your luck.'

'I must see the lions. Especially the male lions. Only the male lions have those beautiful manes,' she'd said.

She hadn't had much luck. She'd only planned to be there for three days, but in the end, she'd cancelled her other travel plans. She stayed on for four more days at the park and, if you counted today, it had already been a full week. Twice a day, he served as her tour guide, telling her about the movements and habits of various animals.

They had seen every animal, except the lions.

Every day, they would take a break at this rest stop. She would buy him a cup of tea and herself a cup of coffee. He would thank her politely every time. This was her way of thanking him, other than paying him for his services and adding a tip.

On the third day, she'd asked why he had chosen to work here.

'Animals are more loveable than people,' he replied. 'Even when they're savage, at least they're openly barbaric.'

On the fourth day, he'd told her that he had a wife who only wanted to live in Cape Town by the coast. Last year, she had asked him for a divorce, as she could no longer stand his passion for nature and wild animals.

On the fifth day, he'd told her that there were once some people who spent the whole day going round the expansive safari grounds but still didn't manage to see a thing. It was when these people had been sitting there, taking a break, that they saw a male lion walk slowly into the grassy plains right before their eyes. The group had just stared in disbelief.

At his story, she had looked in in the direction of the grassy plains.

'I can feel it,' she'd said slowly.

'You can feel it?'

'Yes,' she'd said. 'Male lions are just a feeling.'

On the sixth day, she'd told him that in one day, she would be heading back to her home country.

'Are you disappointed?'

'Maybe it's because I haven't seen a lion yet that I have hope,' she replied.

On the seventh day, they still didn't see any lions. She looked at him walking towards her, holding two cups, curlicues of steam rising into the air.

'You're drinking coffee today?' she asked, surprised.

'Well, today, I'm kind of craving the alertness that coffee

produces.'

'Would lions be kept awake if they drank coffee?' she asked.

He looked like he wanted to say something, but nothing came out of his mouth. She sat facing him, her back to the vast plains. In the quiet afternoon, she could even see the fine stubble on his face as the breeze caressed it gently. For a fleeting moment she saw his eyes gasp in awe. There was no doubt about it—his eyes looked as if they had drawn breath sharply. She didn't ask why but couldn't help admire how he'd used every ounce of effort to let his eyes do the talking and not give anything away in speech.

All she had to do was turn around to see what he saw, but she didn't.

On the return journey, she told him that she would come back after completing some business at home.

'What kind of business?' he asked, hands on the steering wheel.

'I'm going to break off the engagement with my fiancé.'

She had thought it over for the past seven days. It had become clear. If he had refused to accompany her on safari because he was afraid of lions, how could she marry him?

'So you'll be back.'

'Of course. There are lions here.'

THE SEA AND THE CHILD

I head home after work, bulky briefcase in hand. I'm almost at my apartment when I find a child sitting in the stairwell. His eyes are shut, and his hands are clasped around a very, very big seashell that he holds close to his ear. *Whose child is this? Which beach did he get the seashell from?*

On the second day, I see the child still listening to the seashell, as though some wondrous music has washed up in his ears. *Whose child is this?* He smells like the sun and the sea. *Where is this sea?* The seashell even emits a scent reminiscent of faraway lands. I hold on tight to my bulky briefcase when these thoughts, light as a feather, drift into my mind.

On the third day, the child suddenly opens his eyes and smiles when I walk past him. He hands me the seashell. I close my eyes and the wondrous sound of the sea fills my ears. I can hear myself as a child, swimming in a very, very big expanse of blue. The pristine white beach next to the sea stretches on and on, its surface covered with seashells. I can hear a child crying in the seashell. When I open my eyes, the child is still smiling at me. I pick up my bulky briefcase and return the seashell to him.

On the fourth day, the child is no longer there, his huge seashell lying forlorn on the floor. I pick it up, flip it over and realise that the seashell is actually an electronic toy. The battery inside has died. *Who would abandon a toy? When was it that the sky and the sea lost yet another child?* The bulky briefcase carries me back to my apartment after work.

APPEARANCE

The two of them have made a habit of revisiting these happy images.

Under the soft lighting, all the photos exude warmth and joy. The couple delights in the cafe's warm glow; in the special warmth the pictures emanate; in the music playing in the background, bundling them tight, snug as a bug in a rug. They sit in the exact same corner they've always sat in these past few years, heads lowered over the photos, exchanging smiles and words in gentle tones. It's a picture of happiness that even the waiter at the cafe has become accustomed to.

When the three-year old boy smiles, his mother's dimples show faintly on his face.

The eight-year old girl has a confident gaze reminiscent of her father's.

'Take care of those photos, ' the waiter likes to say when he brings their coffee. 'Such beautiful kids! How old were they when you took these?'

The boy is now thirteen. With the lines that have appeared at the corners of his mouth, he is starting to resemble his father again.

The girl is now eighteen. The petals of her youth unfurl like a budding flower. Now that the girl has blossomed into a beautiful young lady, the mother thinks it's very lucky she resembles her more.

As they gaze at these images of their happiness, the waiter also gazes at them basking in happiness. Gradually, he starts to join them in scrutinizing their happiness as he serves them coffee.

'This must be him at twenty-one? Ah, I remember how he looked in that photo of him at three. He had this mischievous smile then. At twenty-one, he has exactly the same smile!'

'And this? Is this really how the little girl looks at thirty? You sure? Thirty?'

All the photos exude warmth and happiness under the soft

lighting. The couple delights in the special warmth the pictures emanate; in the music playing in the background, bundling them snug as a bug in a rug. They've always sat in the exact same corner these past few years, heads lowered over their photos, smiles and words exchanged in gentle tones. Happy times, however, whiz by in the blink of an eye.

When the waiter brings their coffee today, they reveal, very softly, that they will be having their wedding ceremony next month.

'Wow. Congratulations! Finally the day has come. Those pictures, those happy times, they are all going to come true.'

The waiter is envious. They're going to have children who bear a resemblance to the person dearest to each of them. This is exactly how happiness should look: a bit of me in you, a bit of you in me. Computer technology has made it possible for a person to see into a bliss-tinted future. The man and the woman only have to scan photos of themselves and import them into a computer in order to see how their offspring will look at whichever age they fancy.

'I'm really envious of you two,' the waiter always says. 'The way you're able to review your happiness before it all happens? You already know.'

Once the waiter leaves, again, they take out the stack of photo printouts that they have of their future children. As usual, they go over the photos, one by one.

They will walk down the aisle next month. Before they'd decided to get married, they'd gone for a medical checkup. The three different specialists whom they had visited told them the same thing: the woman is infertile.

All the photos exude warmth and happiness under the soft lighting. The couple delights in the special warmth the pictures emanate; in the music playing in the background, bundling them snug as a bug in a rug. This time, however, they see the real face of happiness in their hearts: a bit of me in you, a bit of you in me.

This life, this warm, snug feeling we cradle in our hands, is so blistering to the touch.

SEVENTHDAY AND THE ZOO

'Does Saturday come after Friday?'

'Yeah.'

Does Seventhday come after Saturday?'

'Yeah.'

'Could you take me to Africa on Seventhday, please? I want to see the lions, elephants and giraffes.'

'Sorry, what did you just say?' asks the adult. 'There's no such thing as Seventhday; it's *Sunday*. Also, I'm not free on Sunday. We'll have to wait for you to be a bit older. Then we can find a Sunday to take you to the zoo to see the lions, elephants, and giraffes.'

From then on, Seventhday vanishes into thin air. Like every other person, the boy goes to school, goes to the bus stop, goes to the bathroom, and goes to bed every day, from Monday to Saturday. After Sunday comes Monday. The boy, now a man, goes to work, goes to the bus stop, goes to the bathroom, and goes to bed.

But the boy inside him doesn't stop looking for Seventhday in between the *ding-a-ling* of the school bell and the *tee-cck* of the punch clock. The boy inside continues his search for Seventhday in between flushing the toilet in the morning and underneath the blanket in the night; in between the familiar stars in the sky and unfamiliar pupils in a stranger's eyes.

Many years pass, but the boy never gets to Africa. However, he does go the zoo regularly. On many Seventhdays, the boy even goes there by himself. From a distance, the boy sees silent and roaring creatures, walking leisurely or running wildly, locked up in iron cages or behind fences. Sometimes the boy goes there on his own; sometimes he takes the man along.

'Ah, I didn't know you lower your head to eat the leaves too.'

One time, when the boy brings the man to the zoo, the man can't help but talk to the giraffe out of curiosity. The giraffe looks at him.

'So you're here to fight for leaves to eat too, you inane poet?'

The man cries out in surprise and, together with the boy, falls back on the sofa in front of the Sunday television programme. From then on, Seventhday vanishes like a magician going *poof.* The man feels guilty, and secretly tries to look for Seventhday—the boy's slice of Seventhday that has been gobbled up by that giraffe.

On Monday, Tuesday, Wednesday, and during the rest of the week, the man takes the boy along, dedicated to the search. To everyone else, the man looks like someone who works hard to live, albeit covered in sweat, like any normal person waiting for Sunday to arrive.

LEFT OKAY, OR RIGHT OKAY?

'What?!' he bursts out in fury. 'You want me to say sorry? No!'

'Just a sorry and everything will be okay. Isn't that right?' advises the person in white calmly.

He refuses to give in. 'He's the okay one, not me! He's clearly wrong. Why must I say sorry?'

The person in white wearing a spotless shirt is his superior. When he speaks, he flashes a row of orderly, dazzling white teeth. The gleaming whiteness of his superior gives him the feeling that he is on his side. Over the decades, he has grown used to this pristine-white environment: white sink, white toilet bowl, white urinal, white wall, white tiles. His surroundings are so white, as soon as there's dirt in a crack, he sees it and wipes it off before anyone else notices its presence.

White puts him at ease. He's worn his sparkling white uniform every day for many years now. The uniform is like a part of his body. On his day off, when he doesn't have to wear it, he feels uncomfortable. When he went onstage to receive his award last year, he wore the same white uniform. That time, he even appeared in the newspapers.

'It's true that you aren't in the wrong. But if you don't apologise to him and it gets into the papers, it won't reflect well on you.'

The person in white is well-educated, so whatever he says must be right. This is the logic he's followed all these years: never doubt what the person in white says. Many years ago, the person in white told him that cleaning the public toilets was by no means a lowly task. This particular public toilet wasn't just any public toilet but a toilet frequented by many foreigners. The public toilet's image was also the country's image, so by extension, he was the keeper of the nation's image.

He has kept those words in his mind, as if he is safekeeping an invaluable treasure. In fact, all his energy and thoughts are devoted to keeping the pristine public toilets sparkling clean. Last year, the relevant authorities held a nationwide Public Toilets Hygiene OK Contest in order to prevent the spread of an infectious disease. The public toilet under his charge impressed the jury greatly and won the Most OK Public Toilet award. It was the first time in his life that he'd ever gone onstage to receive an award. At the time, he was awestruck by the person in white's foresight.

'I'm not scared of him! He's the one who'll lose face if this goes to the papers. A grown man like him can't even pee properly. I'm not scared about being in the papers. Not even one bit.'

'Well, I'm not sure if that's a good view to take,' the person in white says in a low voice. 'This foreigner has a relative who works for a news agency. It's very easy for this sort of news to blow up in the foreign media. If that happens, it will be something that concerns not just you but the whole country.'

He continues to insist that he is not at fault.

'But I did nothing wrong! He peed on the floor.'

'Just one drop.'

'One drop of pee is still pee! So yellow some more. Make the white floor dirty! A person wearing suit and tie, and he can't even aim properly into the urinal when he pees!'

'You can mop up the urine after he leaves.'

'Exactly. I was holding my mop, waiting for him to leave.'

'Well, he said you scolded him.'

'I *scolded* him? What? I only said, "Stand in the centre, can aim more properly. Okay or not?"'

'It doesn't sound good. If any foreigner hears this, they'll say we're strait-laced and over-obsessed about cleanliness. They will think that our country micro-manages everything and that we even want to micro-manage the way people stand when they pee.'

'If I don't manage this toilet, who will? I've managed it for so many years already. I don't care what happens outside the public toilet, but if anyone comes in to pee or poo, then I have to do something! Even if the toilet is small, it has its rules. Anyone who breaks the rules is wrong.'

'Just say sorry. Just a sorry will make things okay.'

'He's okay, but I'm not okay.'

'Do it for the country.'

'My country can't make me say I'm wrong when I'm not, okay?'

'Alright. Don't do it for the country, then. Do it for yourself. That person said he's going to sue you.'

'He's *siao* lah. He thinks I'm scared of him?'

'He said that you kept…'

'Keep what?'

'He said…well. He said you kept staring at his whistling birdie.'

'Oh, is it? Yeah, I was looking at it. So? It's the gents. If you're a man, you have to take your birdie out for a whistle, okay? What's the problem here? If I stand there and watch, they won't dare to anyhow stand, anyhow aim, anyhow drip. I study this for a long time already. Your position in front of the urinal must be accurate. If you are too near, too far, aim too left, aim too right, then your pee will spray out of the urinal and dirty the floor. If everyone does that, then our toilet will not be okay anymore.'

'So, here's the problem. He's saying now that if you don't apologise to him, he's going to sue you for sexual harassment.'

'What? I've only heard of men sex harassing women. Is he a woman? I think his brain really not okay. You all better bring him to the doctor for a check-up.'

'Listen. He's a foreigner. They have a different way of thinking. He claims it was a sexual harassment of his consciousness.'

'Hah? What the hell is "sexual harassment of his consciousness"?'

'Think about it. Even though you didn't touch him, your eyes kept staring at his package. Tell me. Were you making sure that he didn't aim left or right? That he should position himself in the centre? I mean, towards the centre?'

'Exactly. I wished I could just—'

'Just use your hand and adjust it for him, right? Your eyes revealed your intention—this is what we call a sexual harassment of the consciousness.'

'I was just concerned about the okayness of the public toilet! What is there to sex harass man to man? That *siao* bastard. If I want to harass, then I harass a woman. I'm normal, okay?'

'Please don't use language like this. We are living in different times. You are now allowed to say that the sexual orientation of some people isn't the same as others in the mainstream society, but you can't say that they aren't normal.'

'Whatever. I'm normal and that's it. I'm not going to say sorry to those foreigners whose heads are not normal.'

The person in white looks at him. He considers for a moment.

'You said you're normal. Are you sure you're one hundred percent normal? Your sexual orientation, I mean.'

'Of course. I don't have money to buy car or house. Look at me. So old and still single. But every time I see a hot and sexy woman, I still get excited.'

'And what else? What else is there to prove that you're normal?'

'I may not be young anymore, but I dream of women all the time. When I wake up in the morning after dreams like that, my cock stands to attention like a soldier.'

The person in white smiles, revealing a row of orderly, dazzling white teeth again.

'You're sure it…stands to attention? Did you ever study your own package carefully?'

'You think I have nothing better to do, is it? I prefer to look at a lady package.'

'Well, did you know? That thing down there that every man has? It's not always straight even if it's standing to attention. Fact is, most people have a tendency to lean to the left or to the right.'

'Is it?'

'You probably don't get to see other people's. How about you have a look at what you have down there tomorrow morning. See if it's totally accurate—I mean, normal—or if it's leaning to the right or left.'

The person in white lowers his voice further and draws closer.

'I have to tell you this. Which way it leans will reveal your sexual orientation. I mean, whether you're into men or not. Your thing down there leaning to the left or right might be all the evidence the foreigner needs to sue you.'

'What? Is this a joke?'

'Just have a very good look at it tomorrow morning, and come see me after. Then you can tell me if you have a hundred percent accurate aim, which will then mean you are one hundred percent okay.'

'Hmm. Can you tell me which will be the problem: right or left?'

The person in white keeps smiling and whispers something into his ear.

'Actually,' he adds after whispering the answer. 'There are many people who lean to the right and there are also many people who lean to the left. People in mainstream society must learn to accept it. It's like you having to tolerate some people who splatter urine on the floor because they aren't standing in the correct position.'

The next day, he goes into the person in white's office, his face red as a beetroot. The person in white blinks.

'So how? Does it lean to the left or to the right?'

He doesn't answer. Reluctantly, he says, 'Fine. I'll say sorry.'

The person in white smiles.

'So everything is okay now, isn't that right?'

TEETH

He hates her teeth with a vengeance.

When she was young, her teeth were her pearly glory. Her skin shone like pearly white teeth; her brows arched like waning crescent moons. But what he loved most was her silver tongue. He couldn't forget how hard she bit into his left chest that moonlit night, saying, 'I hate myself for loving you.'

The bite marks are long gone. But, every time he thinks about it, he feels that ache in his left chest all over again. When she said, 'I do,' in front of the officiator on their wedding day, her smile a dazzling show of teeth, that sweet ache gnawing at his chest had been most palpable.

This woman, whom he had spent half a century of his life with, was always very toothy indeed. But as her age advanced, her pearly shines and crescent moons diminished into nothing but teeth. When midlife opened a new chapter in their life, she would bare her teeth and, like a dictator, order him around day in and day out. *You forgot to turn off the lights! Go take a bath and make it quick!* Every time someone visited, she would wield that razor-sharp tongue of hers and cut him deeply. *I simply can't stand that man! He can't even do a simple thing right like squeezing toothpaste out of the tube!*

Yet, the thing he found most unbearable was her teeth-grinding habit. She would grind her teeth gently, rhythmically and continuously in her sleep. Grinding into his dreams. Very softly, she would grind his slumber, yet not grind it into powder completely. He had been awoken on so many occasions and he'd sit up in bed and look at her, sleeping like a log. He couldn't think of anything other than how this very toothy woman had pulverised his life into fine dust.

During the few days of the funeral, as she lay motionless in the coffin, he started to observe the teeth of all the people who had come to pay their respects. Everyone was more or less obliged to open their mouths—they had to express their condolences at least. He was startled to find himself actually in the mood to study everyone's teeth, so much so that he even discovered how different every person's tooth structure was. Only then did he realise that her teeth had been the only prominent feature in his life in the past few decades. He had eyes for nothing else.

She lay there in the open coffin so everyone could bid her a final farewell. It was the last time they would look at her face, but it was also the very first time she wasn't dictating conversation in the room, or criticise him in front of everyone. She lay there, so refined and dignified. This time, no one had the chance to glimpse into her open mouth and see her teeth.

How long ago was the funeral? Last month? Last year? His memory has become a thick fog. He's been listless lately, probably because he hasn't been sleeping well at night. Now that he doesn't have to go to sleep with the sound of grinding teeth filling up his ears, the nights have become as still as a tomb. What he hears is the endless expanse of silence clouding his ears—a silence so clamorous that he has no restful sleep. Soon after, he realises he has started to grind his teeth.

At first, he doesn't realise he's started doing this. There isn't anyone by his side putting him in his place anymore. Even if his teeth grinding were as loud as thunder, no one would chastise him. It is the sound of him grinding his own teeth that startles him awake. One night, he finds that he can no longer sleep. Sitting up in bed, he takes something out from his bedside table drawer.

They're her dentures. In her later years, she had secretly started to wear partial dentures. She loved to look good, and had warned him to keep it a secret. He managed to keep it from everyone till the very end, though a secret of his very own has sprouted in the confines of strict confidence. Since she could never open her mouth again in front of everyone, he secretly took out her dentures and put them away so that she would leave this world a dignified lady, forever unable to 'bare her teeth'. It was his final act of vengeance.

How many still-as-a-tomb nights have passed? His mind goes over, again and again, how much he hated her teeth on those toothy nights. He holds her teeth in his hand, feeling the ache gnawing at his chest, listening to his memory replaying the familiar sound of teeth grinding. Slowly, he falls asleep. For the past few decades, he has been looking forward to having a good night's sleep. Now that he is holding her teeth in his hand, his wish to have a good sleep has become all the more fervent.

A FUTURE WITHOUT LP

When Sir L appeared at the classroom door, I was playing an idiom card game with my students. I didn't notice him at first. Chen Guohua, the student sitting next to me, said: 'Mr. Han, the TV crew's here again.'

I looked up and knew immediately that it was Sir L. I hurried over to his side and addressed him respectfully. 'My Lord...'

Sir L made a bow with his hands folded in front, just like how people would greet each other in ancient China.

'You're a Chinese teacher, isn't that right, brother? I have three questions I'm hoping you'll be kind enough to give me guidance on. That is, if it's alright with you?'

I received him with due propriety. The students weren't too surprised to see a man from ancient China walking into the classroom. Last month, the TV station sent a crew to our school to film a sci-fi show that features a protagonist hailing from the Qing Dynasty. In the show, he apparently walks into a time tunnel and finds himself in the classroom of a secondary school in post-millennium Singapore. The students were understandably excited when they were roped in to be background actors in the show. We busied ourselves for one whole afternoon filming the scenes that were edited into a few minutes of screen-time.

Sir L was very courteous. He entered the classroom and greeted the students in a bright, booming voice. The students greeted him back with 'good day to you.' Huang Zhiming winked at me, giving me a knowing smile. Zhang Lijuan kept popping her head round the classroom door. She was probably trying to guess where the video camera had been hidden.

I, on the other hand, was elated to see Sir L in person, given how I have adored him since young. My feelings weren't too different from how the students felt last week when their TV idol stood among them in their very own classroom. Sir L looked more weathered and melancholic than the ethereal image I had of him in my mind.

'Here's my first question,' he asked. 'I have so many poems to my name. There must be thousands of them, to say the least. Why do you teach only 'Jing Ye Si'? Is that all you can teach? It makes me feel like I've only written this one poem.'

I didn't know how to answer his question about his poem *Thoughts on a Still Night*, but I managed to mumble something like, 'That's…that's the literary history editor's job.'

The whole class started to recite the verse together:

Chuang qian ming yue guang

Yi shi di shang shuang

Ju tou wang ming yue

Di tou si gu xiang

Sir L's eyes lit up.

'Which one of you can come to the board here and write it for me?' he asked the students.

The students shook their heads. As the dozens of students shook their heads at the same time, I could actually feel a breeze wafting through the classroom.

'Please don't ask the students to write in Chinese,' I whispered to Sir L. 'Don't pressure them unnecessarily.'

Sir L sighed. He used his finger as a marker and wrote down the seven Chinese characters 眼前有景道不得 on the whiteboard, a line from a poem referring to 'an inability to write lines of poetry, even though the beautiful scenery before us warrants it'. The words 'yan qian you jing dao bu de' seemed to have cut through time and space, miraculously materializing before us. The students' thunderous applause resonated across the classroom.

'Wow! Six Meridian Divine Swords! Awesome skill! I saw it on TV,' exclaimed Chen Guohua.

'Interesting, Mr. Han,' Zhang Lijuan piped up in English before continuing in Chinese. 'That time our English lit teacher came to class as Shakespeare, he also recited a poem. Man, I must say, he was no match for this actor that you've invited. This one's so good!'

'He isn't an actor—' I tried to tell the students.

Sir L cut me off.

'Here's my second question. Since you've been teaching my poem 'Jing Ye Si' for such a long time in your classrooms, why hasn't anyone paid me royalties?'

I could feel my face burning up. 'Well, I...actually...um, are you a member of the Copyright Association? Matters regarding copyrights aren't really part of my job scope.'

Zhang Lijuan whispered, 'Mr. Han, can you please tell me where the video camera is?'

Sir L, on the other hand, was not ready to throw in the towel.

'Alright. Here's my last question. I heard that you've removed an essay about me from your secondary school Chinese curriculum. How come?'

Chen Guohua gave me a thumbs up. 'Wow, Mr. Han. I gotta hand it to you. You keep saying, "Less preaching, more learning," but you've outdone yourself and found another way to teach us a banned essay! It's not even part of the course wor! If it turns out to be no fun at all, we'll go complain hor. We'll tell them that you secretly taught us this essay.'

I was overcome with worry. Now my students mistakenly thought I wasn't abiding by the teaching guidelines. I decided to try my best to respectfully ask Sir L to leave. He raised his hand to stop me from opening my mouth and instead asked the concerned student, 'Do you think I'm obsolete? Or do you think I'm irrelevant to the local linguistic landscape? Let me tell you: I'm very in, as you'd say in English. I'll never, ever be obsolete. Isn't being bicultural very *happening* now? I was already representative of bicultural upbringing during my times. Do you want to see me write in Tubo, the language of ancient Tibet?'

'Sir, how about next time...' I tried my best to hint that time was up. Sir L simply wouldn't let it go and continued his lament.

'I understand you want me to be "closer to home". It's all too understandable. I'll let you address me by an English name if that would suit you better? Many years ago, sinologists in the West had already started using the Roman alphabet to address me because they wanted to study my poems. Some people call me Li Po, and some call me Li Pai. To make it simpler for you, you can address me as LP.'

As soon as he said that, the whole class roared with laughter. Chen Guohua kept banging on the table as he guffawed; Zhang Lijuan looked like she was in stitches, patting her tummy as she chortled; Huang Zhiming lost his balance and fell to the floor along with his chair, letting loose another roar of laughter.

I was drowning in an ocean of worry. The boisterous laughter reverberated around the classroom, and there was no way the principal would be spared the hubbub. Therefore, with much resignation, I told Sir L that he had to leave. 'Sir, please go. I'm afraid I don't have an answer to your last question either.'

Sir L looked at my students, who were looking more and more like a bunch of clowns by the minute. He then looked at me. I think he could see his own sorrow in my eyes, like how I could see my sadness in his.

Sir L laughed heartily, taking big confident strides out of the classroom without a care in the world. I looked at his figure disappearing into the distance. His voice, fearless and unrestrained, drifted across the corridor: 'tian sheng wo cai bi you yong...'

As Sir L's famed saying—'There must be some use for my talent.'—faded away, I turned my head and saw Huang Zhiming before me.

'Mr. Han, you've made Chinese lessons more interesting and relaxing now that we don't learn about LP by reading his work. We'll nominate you as the most creative Chinese teacher this year.'

I didn't say a word. Instead, I lowered my head and continued to play the idiom card game with my students. I'd spent a whole month designing those cards.

The LP memorandum: In September 2004, S City's Foreign Minister appealed to the United Nations General Assembly to stop the conflict between two places. The Foreign Minister of one of those places, T Island, said in a speech that S City is 'a country the size of a booger'. He then added in Hokkien (Taiwanese dialect) slang that S City 'embraces the LP of another country'. That caused an uproar among the global media, with T Island's citizens requesting that their government issue an apology to S City, as 'LP' in Hokkien refers to the male sexual organ. The relentless media reports on the issue made it sound even more offensive, especially when they couldn't find an appropriate word in Mandarin to replace the Hokkien word in time. Therefore, in follow-up reports and commentaries, the media decided to go with the term 'LP', which they had used in the breaking news report. Subsequently, the term 'LP' filled the radio airwaves, TV broadcast, newspapers and internet. From then on, 'LP' took on a new meaning among the many English acronyms, and became 'the original definition'. A generation of overseas Chinese now has a collective memory of LP.

NOTES ON THE WIND FROM GRANDPA AND PA'S CHILDHOOD

1.

The buffalo lowers its head to eat the grass. The buffalo makes no sound, and the grass makes no sound. Behind the buffalo is a paddy field, and behind the paddy field, the green hills, and behind the green hills, the blue skies. In the blue, blue skies, there are white, white clouds. The paddy field doesn't make a single sound. The green hills, blue skies and white clouds have never uttered a single word. Only when the wind blows in my direction, do I hear its hushed whisper.

To this day, every time the wind blows, I can still hear the sounds of childhood and a buffalo eating grass.

2.

The buffalo lowers its head to eat the grass. Behind the buffalo is a paddy field, and behind the paddy field, the green hills, and behind the green hills, the blue skies. In the blue, blue skies, there are white, white clouds. The buffalo, the grass, the green hills and the white clouds have never uttered a single word. They reside in a painting hanging on the living room wall. This painting, my Pa said, is a reproduction of the childhood that he had in his hometown, conjured up bit by bit from memory.

To this day, every time I think of my Pa's painting, I hear the sound of my own childhood, and what I imagine to be the sound of a buffalo eating grass.

3.

The buffalo lowers its head to eat the grass. Behind the buffalo is a paddy field, and behind the paddy field, the green hills, and behind the green hills, the blue skies. In the blue, blue skies, there are white, white clouds. The buffalo, the grass, the green hills and the white clouds are all lurking on my screensaver without making a single sound. Every time I switched on the computer, I would see that buffalo.

My Pa told me it was a buffalo. That was my very first computer—a birthday present that Pa bought me on my seventh birthday. Pa added that he'd taken the photo of Grandpa's painting with his digital camera, lest I miss out on the wonderful childhood he and Grandpa once had. Not only that, he had even set up sounds of the wind blowing across the field for me. I only had to press the button on my mouse lightly and the sound of the wind blowing across Grandpa and Pa's childhood would come drifting from the computer.

To this day, when I visit the unfamiliar factory in China on a company work trip and see a buffalo in the countryside lowering its head to eat the grass, tears roll down my cheeks like when I saw one for the very first time. The summer wind blows gently across the field. In my heart a wound bleeds, opening up a raw and tender yearning at the memory of the day my computer crashed. I was ten then, and I had to bid it goodbye forever, along with my childhood which went crashing with it—long, long ago.

HERE COMES THE ELEPHANT

Her son was only six and loved telling fibs.

She'd told him the story of *The Boy Who Cried Wolf* before: there was once a shepherd boy who was bored to death herding sheep in the mountains. One day he cried, 'Wolf! Wolf!', sending everyone into a frenzy. Their concern later turned into rage after they realised that there was no wolf—the boy had told a big, fat lie. After that, when a wolf really did arrive, no one came to save the sheep even when the boy screamed himself hoarse. In the end—she said in an emphatic tone—the wolf ate the boy as well.

'Do you understand?' she asked the boy gravely. The boy nodded. His eyes widened and he pointed out of the window. 'Wolf!'

Her son must be fibbing because he was bored. It was an attempt to get his mother's attention. She had too much on her plate. Even though she worked from home, she was always on the computer buried in her translation work. Her child would sit by the tall glass window looking out at the street.

'Mama, lion walk by.'

Her eyes were fixed on the computer.

'Is that so?'

'Mama, downstairs, hippo walk by. Is so cute.'

'Ok, sweetie. Draw it for me later, ok?' Her eyes were still on the screen. She was far too preoccupied to turn her head to talk to her child.

Today, the child said there was a 'xiang' downstairs.

'Do you remember the story that Mama told you, sweetie?'

'But Mama, is real xiang downstairs.'

'Hmm. Okay. I'll come take a look in a bit.'

She finally finished her article translation. She stretched her whole body and stood up, walked over to the window, and took a look at her child. His face was veiled in disappointment.

'Do you remember Mama telling you why we shouldn't fib?'

She cast a look out of the window, looking very hard at the street downstairs. 'Where's the xiang you saw?' she said.

'There is real xiang, a baixiang! But someone come and now is gone.'

'Is that so?' She looked in exasperation at her child who was fibbing without even batting an eyelid.

The next day, her friend called her and asked if she had read the papers. It seemed there was a white elephant in her neighbourhood yesterday.

'Sorry, did you just say "white elephant", like a "baixiang"?' She looked at her computer screen, her headphones covering her ears. 'Look, I'm trying to meet a deadline now. Let's talk later.'

After she finished her article, she told her child that her friend had called.

'Auntie called. She said that there really was a baixiang in our neighbourhood yesterday, so you did see one walking by! You didn't lie, Mama was wrong. Next time when there's a lion, hippo or xiang walking by, you tell Mama, ok?'

On another day, when she was working on her computer, her son looked out the window again.

'Mama, is MRT downstairs! Is coming. Coming here.'

She stopped what she was doing and went to the window in excitement. She held her child in her arms, and the two of them looked happily at the MRT downstairs. They looked at the train rumbling by for a very, very long time until she woke up. This time, her son didn't say anything about the xiang. Her dream told her a story so real, so palpable, that it was literally 'zhenxiang'.

White Elephant Prologue: In August 2005, a Minister of Parliament from S City visited a constituency. The construction of an MRT underground train station had long been completed, but the station was never put in operation. The neighbourhood residents made an appeal but without success. When the minister was due to visit one day, someone had put a cardboard white elephant on the roadside. The 'white elephant' was hastily cleared away, as the person who put it there did not apply for a license or have one approved, thus breaking the public entertainment and assembly law. Someone reported the incident to the police, prompting them to look into the matter. The media was hot on the heels of this 'White Elephant Incident', and the Transport Minister was alerted.

White Elephant Epilogue: In mid-November 2005, when this book was being proofed, the Transport Minister announced that the MRT station mentioned in the story would be in operation in mid-January 2006. The news headline was 'From White Elephant to Reality', or in Chinese, 'From Baixiang to Zhenxiang'.

UNFINISHED

It was a Sunday when I walked into Grandpa's room, intending to give it a proper clear-out. As soon as I stepped in, I seemed to see Grandpa sitting in his armchair again, his words fresh in my ears.

'Don't go messing with my things,' Grandpa would always mumble as he sat in his armchair, the sunlight pouring in like golden honey through the window, softly illuminating the right side of his face, sketching out its contours as his lips moved up and down.

After completing Grandpa's funeral arrangements, I had put off going into his room for a whole week. Even though the door had been kept tightly shut during the last few days, I couldn't shake off the feeling that he was inside—that the two of us still lived and breathed together in this house.

I was only nineteen, still doing my National Service, when my parents died in a car accident. Grandpa and I had looked after each other for nearly ten years since their deaths.

Ailments that come with old age kept Grandpa in his room most of the time. His eyesight had also deteriorated in recent years, making it even harder for him to leave his room, or his armchair, a gift that I'd bought him with my first pay cheque.

He'd muttered that I was a sor zai when I gifted him that chair, chiding me for being a silly boy spending money on unnecessary things, especially when the armchair wasn't even comfortable. Yet, from that day on, it became an integral part of his life, like a body that held him close, keeping him warm and snug as he leaned into its soft embrace and slowly became one with it as the years went by.

Now, I sank my whole body into the armchair, trying to imagine how Grandpa used to fall into its firm backrest and steady arms on those twilight evenings: all hushed and serene, his eyes gently closed. The way his body would retreat into relaxation, the way his face would withdraw into contentment as he listened intently to the radio broadcasting the evening news in Cantonese.

A few of those times I'd stood close by, silently taking in his expression. He would open his eyes suddenly and say, 'You're here to check if I've stopped breathing, aren't you?'

I'd laugh and say, 'I'm here to see if you've fallen asleep.'

Grandpa always replied, 'Sor zai, I can't sleep when the news is on. We've only got five minutes of Cantonese news every day. I can't fall asleep and miss it.'

Grandpa never spoke in Mandarin. If anyone spoke to him in Mandarin, he refused to reply. After my parents died, I attempted to converse with him in broken Cantonese. Even if those attempts were inept, they were a surprisingly good way to improve my Cantonese, as Grandpa never hesitated to comment on my inaccurate pronunciation.

My father once confided in me that Grandpa had now withdrawn into himself. After walking became more and more difficult for him, his only solace was listening to the Cantonese news in the evening.

Once I knew this, I made sure to turn on the radio for him every day according to the evening broadcast schedule. It was hard for him to reach it with his failing sight. If I had to be out, I would set the radio to turn on automatically, so that Grandpa would still be able to rest in his armchair, listening to the Cantonese news that provided his daily stimulation on the dot.

Today, as I sat reminiscing in Grandpa's armchair, it became clear to me that his passing was inevitable: old age took him away, and my brooding over it wouldn't change a thing. He had actually extended his time in this world by a year, which should leave me with no more regrets.

*

A year ago, Grandpa's condition took a turn for the worse. His debilitating health coincided with the announcement that news broadcasts in Chinese dialects—including Cantonese—would be terminated in a month. This historic termination didn't sit too well with Grandpa. When he heard the announcement, he sighed and voiced his dismay in between coughs: 'Just a month left. Just one more month to listen to my Cantonese news, and then I'm going to have to leave this world.'

As Grandpa's health continued to decline, I was more and more anxious to keep him upbeat. I struggled to string my reassurances together in coherent Cantonese: 'Perhaps the radio station will change its mind, Grandpa. I can always buy more Cantonese CDs for you to listen to.' But Grandpa kept silent, shaking his head.

As luck would have it, glad tidings arrived two weeks after the termination announcement. The radio station, during one of its Cantonese news segments, announced that it would be postponing its dialect news termination as many people had petitioned against it. In a strange turn of events, Grandpa's health was also restored, as was the Cantonese news. I thought to myself then, those five minutes of Cantonese news a day were better than any elixir in the world.

*

One year has since flown by.

Just ten days ago, I found Grandpa's body motionless in the armchair. His breathing had come to a halt. The news announced its presence in Cantonese as usual, but Grandpa's eyes were shut tight. He had, however, set his mouth in an upward crescent, gifting me my only gleam of consolation.

As the memories came flooding back, a fervent desire arose in me to relive all those days of Grandpa sitting in his armchair, listening to the Cantonese news. My sight fell upon the radio, which I had tucked away in an inaccessible spot.

I reached into my pocket and took out a cassette tape, intending to put it into the radio that had faithfully played, and recorded, numerous segments of Cantonese news for Grandpa. I had become a master in this for the past year.

It was then that I felt a lump in Grandpa's pillow. Something was underneath.

Moving the pillow aside, I saw a box of cassette tapes different from those that I had used. Out of curiosity, I played one of these tapes instead, and was surprised to hear Grandpa's voice.

'Sor zai, so you think Grandpa doesn't know how to turn on the radio myself? You really think I don't know that you made up the news and recorded them in Cantonese? Your youngest uncle always pronounces the "Heung" in "Heung Gong" differently; he keeps sounding like he's saying "Hung". Just that strange pronunciation alone already tells me that he's the one reading the news.'

Oh my, Grandpa *was* smart. I'd thought I'd outsmarted him, but he was the one with the wits. Even my youngest uncle had been fooled.

This youngest uncle of mine had been estranged from the family as a youth when Grandpa kicked him out of the house after they'd fought. My dad used to see him secretly, but when he died in the accident, I continued their tradition and stayed in touch with my uncle.

My uncle was indifferent when I approached him to record the news for Grandpa. Firmly declaring that he didn't want to have anything to do with him, Uncle went as far as to say that he wouldn't even be attending Grandpa's funeral when he someday passed on. But despite his vehement refusal, he succumbed to my pleas and grudgingly agreed to do the recordings. He turned out to be so committed that even I fell short by comparison—looking for a voice changer, taking pains to revise the Mandarin news script into Cantonese. Unfortunately, all that zeal only fit into the span of a year. Uncle exited from the recordings when he exited from life: lung cancer took him away last month. Just as he'd prophesied, he really didn't pay his last respects at Grandpa's funeral.

However, he had managed to rush out a whole month's worth of news recordings in his remaining days. The content was made up: the Singaporean government considering the reinstatement of dialect TV programmes, a happy reconciliation between China and Taiwan. They were all the good news that Grandpa had wished for. The news recording that I would have played today for him would have been the very last one that Uncle recorded, but Grandpa left before he had the chance to hear it.

My fingers ran over the radio set and clicked play. The news came on and the familiar intonations of Uncle's newscaster voice filled the room. An uncertainty suddenly overcame me: was I grieving the loss of Uncle or Grandpa? Perhaps I was just clinging on to memories of being Grandpa's sor zai?

In the background, the news announced: *Our Cantonese news broadcast will take a break from tomorrow onwards, but rest assured, it will resume very soon. Stay tuned.*

I stayed seated in Grandpa's armchair, listening to the Cantonese news that he didn't manage to hear. It then occurred to me that the smile on Grandpa's face when he breathed his last breath was a response to Uncle's voice over the radio; in the end, Uncle did pay his last respects to Grandpa. As his voice flitted into my ears, I caught Uncle mispronouncing the Cantonese word 'Heung' in Hong Kong as 'Hung' again.

Grandpa's smile sneaked onto my face, unravelling itself like an untold secret that we were both privy to.

THE JOY OF A LEFT HAND
(Almost an Afterword)

A few years ago, I went travelling in France with my wife. We took the train from Nice in the south to Lyon in central France. On the train, we met a French man who spoke fluent English. When we reached Lyon, he invited us to his place for dinner. This man was an author who had a few books to his name, and one of them had even won a national literary award.

As we were both authors, we had quite a few things in common to talk about. For the past few years, we've kept in correspondence and he emails me his new work as attachments. I'm one of his first readers. Occasionally, I also email him my feedback.

Recently, he sent me a story that he said was not written by him but his friend. His friend had never published a book, or any literary writings for that matter, so he wanted my opinion on whether his friend's story was worth publishing. He translated the story into English and emailed it to me. I subsequently translated it into Chinese, and it goes like this:

There was once a man who looked like everyone else, except he had a secret. This secret had been hidden inside him for so long that he would, at times, forget what it was.

He was born a left-hander. But he barely remembered it by the time he reached adulthood.

When he was young, his mother had tried very hard to teach him how to use his right hand to open the door, switch on the lights, and turn on the tap. His father taught him how to use his right hand to write, sign his name, and shake hands with another person. He had always been a smart child. His kindergarten teacher had remarked, 'He learns everything fast and well.' His primary school teacher had written in his report card, 'Delightful and popular with everyone.'

The boy, on the surface, grew up in the same way as every other boy. It's just that he couldn't remember that he was born a left-

hander. He was thirteen when he accidentally used his left hand for the first time. He was taking a shower in the bathroom and, for the first time, became very excited about a particular part of his body. His curiosity got the better of him, and he couldn't keep his left hand off it. At that very moment, his father opened the bathroom door and walked in. Afterwards, his father gave him a solemn talking to in the study, telling him that boys would naturally want to do what he had done once they were older. However, he should not indulge in the act, especially not with his left hand. He should always use his right one instead.

When he was twenty, he was fooling around with his first love in a car. Excitedly, he unbuttoned his girlfriend's blouse and explored her body with his fingers. His girlfriend closed her eyes and cried out his name softly. Suddenly, she opened her eyes and looked at him with surprise. 'Why are you using your left hand?'

He was thirty when he used his left hand for the last time. For the very first time in his life he decided, on the spur of the moment, to go to the polling station to cast his vote on Polling Day. He wanted to be a law-abiding citizen and vote for the ruling party, so he had no idea why he made a mark in the opposition party's box instead. When he was about to submit the ballot paper, a voice from the PA system overhead said, 'Sir, voting for the opposition party isn't a problem at all. However, only votes made with the right hand are counted as a vote.' It was then that he realised that he had been using his left hand.

A few years went by. Like everyone else, he entered midlife. People who knew him said that he was the perfect husband, father, colleague and friend.

One day, he woke up very early to find the rest of his family still asleep. When he left the house, the dog was still asleep too. Very quietly, he left his familiar housing estate, his familiar city. As the sun was rising, he came to a grassy field on a hill on the city outskirts.

He was all alone, except for the rustling of the wind and the swaying of the grass. He sat down and looked over to the other side of the hill. No one saw (if there was anyone there at that point in time) what he was looking at. He sat down after that, stretched out his trembling left hand, which he no longer had mastery of, and slowly proceeded to do something private.

He wrote a story. The story began like this: A few years ago, I went travelling in France with my wife. We took the train from Nice in the south to Lyon in central France. On the train, we met a French man who spoke fluent English.

I've been hesitating about writing an afterword for this collection. D.H Lawrence once said, 'Never trust the teller; trust the tale.' (Did Lawrence really say that? Do you believe me?) It's best that novelists do not talk about what they have written, but I would like to share with you why this book is titled *The Joy of a Left Hand*.

Milan Kundera once said that he didn't like to use ornamental metaphors in his writing, preferring only to use conceptual metaphors. If he had to use a metaphor, that metaphor had to be the climax of the story (after writing this, out of habit, my right hand almost wanted to cite a source and specific edition. However, when I thought about how serious an annotation would look, I decided against it).

I have always been writing essays, poems and song lyrics with my right hand (please don't ask me if this is a metaphor), and the more I write with my right hand, the more natural it is to write with my right hand (this is what Susan Sontag objects to, and also what critics like to explain as 'out of habit'). As I have been writing with my right hand for the longest time, I almost forgot that my very first compositions were imagined 'stories', written in a children's exercise book.

I can't remember when it was that I started to miss how artless I was as a young writer. I miss the simplicity and pure happiness inherent in that state of naiveté. Therefore, very quietly and very clumsily, I started to use my left hand to write things that were unfamiliar; things that carried the appearance of the unknown, untouched, uncommon. Sometimes, these things are so strange compared to what I usually write that my right hand is shocked. Sometimes, I feel very happy that I am using my left hand to write again.

Sometimes, I suspect that all authors are secret left-handers (this is definitely a metaphor). They help reclaim left-hander stories from the pragmatic right-handers.

Support from my mentors and fellow writer friends have made me—a left-handed author—less lonely in this world so dominated by the right hand.

Last but not least, I'd like to share two things. Firstly, I've never been to France. Secondly, I'm not a left-hander. Which one is fact, which one is fiction? Is this afterword a (fictional) short story, or is it an (factual) essay? Are you still asking? Yes, you, whom I've been conjuring up in my mind. You, my reader, who have been reading this in earnest.